· A · Cockeyed Guide to the Hamptons

Reynolds Dodson

Illustrations by

Laura Hartman Maestro

A Cockeyed Guide to the Hamptons

Library of Congress Control Number: 2010917355
CIP data is available.

Text set in Granjon
Illustrations © 2010 by Laura Hartman Maestro
Designed by Victoria Hartman
Printed in the United States of America

ISBN-10: 1453751408

To Steve Jobs and Bill Gates,

without whom I would have had

to do this on a typewriter

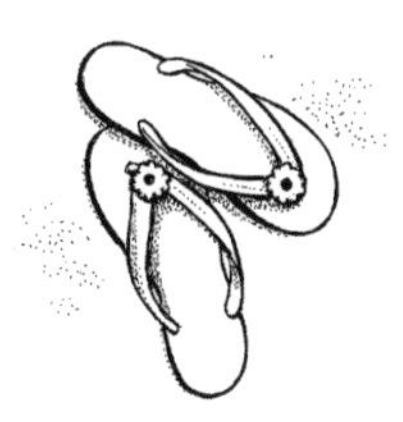

A Cockeyed Guide to the Hamptons

Introduction

In 1640, Governor John Winthrop of Massachusetts dispatched a small group of English settlers to establish a colony on Long Island. Presumably he wanted them to build a place where the Dutch could hang out on weekends and buy t-shirts. After all, life in Manhattan is so stressful.

The settlement they founded was called Southampton, and it was sufficiently pleasant that it became the model for other settlements. Soon, Baby Hamptons were sprouting up all along the island's lower mandible, and upon the arrival of the railroad, closely followed by Puff Daddy, the Fabulous Hamptons were born.

The Hamptons are a kind of schizoid place where life is lived on parallel planes. There are the Hamptons as experienced by weekenders and reported in the New York City press, and then there are the Hamptons as experienced by those who actually live here. The two have nothing in common.

Not long ago, there was an article in the Sunday Styles section of *The New York Times* that described life in the Hamptons this way: "The Hamptons wants you to perceive it as conforming to the spirit of these times and not to caricature it as the flashy, traffic-choked, over-the-top playground it has increasingly become. Low-key is the theme this year, no matter how much it costs."

Frankly, I was surprised to hear that "the Hamptons" wanted you to perceive it as anything. If they had asked me, I would have said, "The Hamptons wants you to perceive it as a place to drive slowly, go to bed early and not make too much noise. It would also help if you turned off your cell phone."

This led me to wonder, Who makes these rules? Is there some sort of committee that sits around all winter and plans how Hampton summers will go? If so, I wish they'd tell me. I had been planning a high-key season. I had to change all my plans.

Believe me, I am not one of those who hates city people, although they can be rather difficult. The fact is, I was once a city person myself, shameful as that may be. I was a man who only came out on weekends and didn't pay a whole lot of attention to what was going on from Monday through Friday. But once I decided to live here fulltime, my attitude changed. For the fact is, visiting here and living here are two different things. For visitors, these are the Hamptons. For year-rounders, this is the East End.*

Perhaps at this point some background is in order. I am not by birth a Long Islander, or even a New Yorker. I was born in Cincinnati, which is nowhere near the Hamptons. The son of an actuary who could never understand my innumeracy (if the course had a number in it, I'd flunk it), I took up writing in self-defense.

I had a happy, unstructured childhood in which I spent most of my time daydreaming, throwing stones at trees and bombing ants with golf balls. That's what kids did in those days. My idea of a play date was to stick my head out the door, ask my friend if he could come out and play, and if he did, throw a stone at him. I can't imagine growing up any other way.

---

*Or more precisely, the South Fork of the East End. If you look at a map, you'll see that Long Island is shaped like an alligator facing east away from New York. It has its mouth open. Its upper jaw is the North Fork and its lower jaw is the South Fork. That little wad of chewing gum in its mouth is Shelter Island. Together, these areas make up the East End, but in this book only the South Fork counts because that's the only place people talk about.

It never occurred to me that I would end up living on the East End. Like most Midwesterners, I didn't even know where Long Island was and in fact grew up with a preternatural prejudice against Easterners. I thought all Easterners were obnoxious Ivy League snobs. Since then, I've learned that that's not true. Only some Easterners are obnoxious Ivy League snobs. Others are just obnoxious. (Only kidding, folks.)

When I was young, if you had asked me to draw a map of the East, it would have looked something like the famous *New Yorker* cover depicting a New Yorker's view of the United States. Only mine would have been from the opposite direction. It would have shown Boston, New York, and Philadelphia somewhere out there beyond Pittsburgh, and in between would have been a couple of ski trails connecting Harvard with the Liberty Bell. As for Long Island, I hadn't the foggiest idea where that was.

Even today, when I tell Midwestern friends that I live a hundred miles east of New York City, they look at me as if I'm crazy. No one can live a hundred miles east of New York City. Nothing exists a hundred miles east of New York City. I might as well tell them I'm living in the Outer Hebrides.

As fate would have it, after college and the army I landed a job at *Reader's Digest*, which was not on Long Island but was in the East. It was in Westchester County, which was also not near the Hamptons. It was an educational experience, but a poor match. Although back then the *Digest* was the world's largest, and by some measures most influential, magazine, its politics were antediluvian, and after being grilled one day on why I didn't have an American flag decal on my car I decided I'd had enough.

I made my way to Manhattan, where I worked for several other magazines and after awhile met my wife, Susan. Susan had a small weekend house in Water Mill, and that's how I came to know the East End.

When we were finally able to enlarge the house and move out full-time, I threw myself into as many activities as possible, most of which annoyed the local politicians.

The politics on the East End are no more inept than anywhere else—they just seem that way. For years, the entire area was controlled by the Republican Party, and although that has changed to some degree, there are still more Republicans here than anything else. But they are not your average Republicans. They do not run on platforms of gay-bashing or repealing Roe v. Wade. Some of them are actually personable.

There are three kinds of people on the East End: locals, year-rounders and weekenders. (There's actually a fourth type called the daytrippers, but we don't talk about them. We just take their money.) Although I have lived here for several decades, I will never be a local. In fact, given the deep-seated traditions of the East End, I'm not sure the locals are locals. Your lineage has to go back to the dinosaurs.

Since I arrived here, the tenor of life in the Hamptons has changed quite noticeably. That's not because of my arrival, but because of all the Wall Street money and crass behavior. Too often, the weekenders act like orangutans. "Citiots" is what the locals call them.

Sometimes this citiocy makes news. Back in 2001, a New York publicity agent named Lizzie Grubman took revenge on one of our local nightclubs by ramming her SUV into their customers. Apparently, she didn't like the way she had been treated. This upset the locals, who thought it exemplified how New Yorkers felt about them. But of course that's not true. Lizzie would have been just as happy mowing down a group of New Jerseyites.

Lizzie was just demonstrating the attitude shown by *The New York Times* and other metropolitan media, albeit in a more violent fashion. The big New York dailies believe that in the

Hamptons weekenders are the only ones who count, and the people who live here are supernumeraries in a show put on by and for the heirs of Brooke Astor.

Imagine for a moment if *The New York Times* reported on life in Manhattan the way they report on life in the Hamptons. It would be from the perspective of people visiting from Keokuk. Their only interest would be the Statue of Liberty and knowing how long the lines are at *The Lion King*. And it's interesting to note to whom these publications turn for information. They never ask anyone who's actually in charge of anything. They never ask one of our town supervisors or our state assemblyman or even a farm stand owner. They only ask nightclub impresarios, real estate agents and Jerry Della Femina, without whom they would be flying blind.

The people who come here on weekends are truly strangers in a strange land. I once met a fellow at a charity event who said he had a house out here on a road with the word "Mecox" in it, but he had no idea which road that was. He had to ask his wife.

I don't think most weekenders could name a single local farmer or garage mechanic if their lives depended on it. If you asked them who their town supervisor is, they'd say Christie Brinkley.

On the other hand, the local East End papers, such as the one I write for, tend to be perversely indifferent to weekenders and exist almost exclusively for the benefit of people who hate summer visitors. Not for them the travails of Mariah Carey or Alec Baldwin. They don't even like the word Hamptons. For them, weekenders and summer renters are just nuisances to be tolerated for the sake of the revenue they bring in through real estate advertising.

As a consequence, most weekenders don't read *The Southampton Press* or any of the other local papers. If anything, they just skim the South o' the Highway section of *Dan's Papers*, which gives them all the information they need.

Over the course of my time here, I have written more than five hundred columns, most of which have been good for nothing but to wrap the next day's garbage. But now and then I've written something that still seems relevant, and these are what I've tried to revisit here.

In gratitude, I'd like to thank Joe Louchheim, publisher of *The Press*; Joe Shaw, *The Press's* Executive Editor; and Peter Boody, *The Press's* former editor, who first gave me a try. Finally, I'd like to thank my wife and my two West Highland terriers, MacDuff and the late great Tucker Himself, both of whom contributed mightily to this effort.

But now to the matter at hand. We'll start with some general observations about the East End, then move on to wherever the current takes us. Buckle up. It could be a choppy ride.

—Reynolds Dodson

Reynolds' Muse

Namesakes

There's something un-American about the East End. In the rest of the country, when children grow up they often pack up their bags and leave. A boy from Cleveland moves to Los Angeles; a girl from Memphis flees to Chicago. Not here.

Here, one is struck by how many families bear the same names as the earliest settlers, the people who arrived in the 17th Century. Obviously, something has kept these families rooted despite hurricanes, depressions, nematodes and car traffic. Even those who leave never leave for long. They're constantly pulled back, like lures reeled in from the surf.

I look at these families as a kind of European royalty, Long Island-style. Those who bear the names Halsey, Herrick and Hildreth seem to comprise a gentry whose sense of responsibility exceeds that found elsewhere. In return for the privilege of being able to drive on roads that bear their names, they uphold the steadfast traditions of an area whose soil won't let them go.

I may be star-struck, but these people seem to me to be better than we interlopers who traipse around in our duck-bill hats and designer t-shirts. I suspect it would seem unthinkable for a Raynor or a Rogers to dress that way. It would be a betrayal of ancestry.

Sometimes I fantasize that the Toppings, Fosters and Sayres meet in secret sessions to exchange news and look with wonder upon what the rest of us are doing. "Who *are* these people," I imagine them saying, "and where do they come from?" We newcomers have arrived with our Porches and BMWs, our lawyers and our architects, building outlandish structures and polluting their ponds, while the original families suffer in silence. It's as if Andy Capp had won the lottery and moved next-door to Queen Elizabeth.

I imagine these families feeling not unlike the Indians who watched their prized lands being turned into freeways and mini-malls. They're saying, "What did we do to deserve this?" Yet, as much as I grieve for them, I also envy them. No matter how much I might love this place, I know I can never do for it what the Barkers, Bishops and Bostwicks have done. It's no secret that, in Water Mill anyway, where I live, when there's work to be done or money to be raised, the volunteers most likely to do it will be Halseys, Squires or Corwiths. Like the Rockefellers, these families seem to have a sense of public service to the community that feeds them.

Sometimes I wonder if, like royalty, they're forced to intermarry. When a Hildreth comes of age, must a suitable partner be found among the Herricks? Is there a mad search among the Roses, Strattons and Whites to find a proper mate for their offspring without thinning the blood or risking hemophilia?

And if that's true, do the Posts and Jessups live in fear that all they have built will be jeopardized by some local equivalent of Princess Fergie?

I suspect it must be difficult to be born into one of these families and know that one can never have the same freedom as other Americans. You can't just take off and become a salmon fisherman in Alaska or a surfer in Baja. Honor demands that you stay here and serve the land of your forbears.

I imagine it may be tempting for these families to do what aristocrats did in old Restoration comedies, slipping into disguise now and then and dropping in on places like Bobby Van's or The Driver's Seat, pretending to be just another weekender putting the make on some winsome barmaid. But, just as in those comedies, it's inevitable that they would be found out, with all the hilarious consequences.

Still, there are many of us who would give anything to trade places with these people, even if it did mean having to act more responsibly than the huggermuggers who carouse in nightclubs or fill the police blotter every week. I for one would love to feel so close to my ancestors and see my name on every other sign in town. It would help me feel legitimized.

Some have hopes of reincarnation and that in another life they'll come back as a king or a lion or a rock star. Not me. When I come back, I hope it's as a Halsey. Then I'll know I'm close to Nirvana.

Spelling Lessons

You may have wondered, as I have, about the quixotic spellings on the East End. For example, why is Southampton spelled with one word and East Hampton with two?

It's a legitimate question. Breathes there a soul who has not paused in mid-envelope and said, "Wait a minute! Should I spell East Hampton with one word or two? And if with two, have I been misspelling Southampton all these years?"

That will lead you to worry about Bridgehampton (Bridge Hampton?), Westhampton (West Hampton?), and all the other Hamptons (Otherhamptons?). Then you'll fret over Water Mill (Watermill?), and how to pronounce Yaphank (Yaffank?). By four in the morning you'll be wondering why Pittsburgh is spelled with an h and Remsenburg isn't.

Let's consider the possibilities.

Perhaps East Hampton is spelled with two words because of the hard consonant on the end of "East". If you spelled it with one word, people might pronounce it "Eess Thampton". (My wife used to pronounce Yaphank "Yaffank", so you see the kind of ignorance we're up against.) No one would want to live in a town called "Eess Thampton". They'd be conthidered thithies.

But that begs the question, Why is Westhampton spelled with one word when it too has a hard consonant at the end of the first syllable? Shouldn't it be pronounced "Wess Thampton"?

You see the problem. The deeper one delves, the murkier it gets. What, for example, does the word "hampton" mean, and does it have any bearing on our towns' spelling?

According to the most learned research available (meaning an article I once read in *Dan's Papers*), "hampton" is a compound of two Old English words, "ham" and "tun", the former meaning "pasture" and the latter meaning "settlement".

That means that Southampton is a settlement on a pasture to the south. To the south of what, no one knows, and it would probably be impolitic to ask.

And yet, according to Abigail Fithian Halsey's book, *In Old Southampton*, our town was probably not named after the British town of Southampton at all, but rather after the Earl of Southampton, he being some big shot who occupied about the same social position as Donald Trump does today. It was an obvious attempt to suck up.*

You will note that there was no Earl of East Hampton or Bridgehampton. This would indicate that those villages are mere knock-offs and undeserving of serious consideration. But before you jump to that conclusion, you have to consider the question of

*And aren't we lucky they were not trying to impress the Earl of Sandwich?

capitol letters. If you live in East Hampton, you get *two,* so might that make you better?

I think a convincing case can be made for the opposite. Note that the modern way of naming things is to run all the words together and put the capitals in the middle. That's how you get PowerBook, ConocoPhillips and USAir.

This suggests that if the original settlers had been way cool, they would have told Governor Winthrop, "Guv, we've just founded SoutHampton [SouthHampton?], and now we're going out to found EastHampton, BridgeHampton and WestHampton."

The guv would have said, "Awesome, dudes! Tweet me when you're back."

Summer Rental FAQs

Every year, when the "Summer Rental" signs come out, status-conscious New Yorkers face the all-important decision of choosing where to rent. To make their lives easier, here are answers to some of the most frequently asked questions.

But before we get to that, you should ask yourself whether you even want to rent out here, or if you're qualified. After all, the Hamptons have their standards. So take this little test and see if you measure up. If you don't, you might want to reconsider and look for something nice in, say, Sheepshead Bay.

Do you own a cell phone?

Of course you do, so give yourself 5 points.

Do you use your cell phone in restaurants and buses?

Probably, so give yourself 15 points.

Do you talk on the cell phone while driving?

If you answered yes to this, give yourself 25 points and submit your name to the Suffolk County Board of Elections. You may be eligible for the George Guldi Golden Yakker Award. This is an award named after a former county legislator who distinguished himself first by loudly and profanely flouting the hands-free cell phone laws, then by running several mortgage scams involving local properties and sex clubs in New York. He is currently facing a stretch in the slammer, but his memory lives on.

Do you drive a Mercedes, Land Rover or BMW?

Give yourself 20 points.

Do you wear a baseball cap backward?

Give yourself 25 points.

Do you wear your baseball cap backward indoors or while driving a Mercedes, Land Rover or BMW?

Give yourself 50 points.

Do you smoke cigars?

Give yourself 40 points.

Do you swear a lot and say "go" when you mean "said"?

Give yourself 30 points.

Do you have no idea where Flanders is?

Give yourself 20 points.

Is your only knowledge of Group for the East End their annual June gala?

Give yourself 25 points.

Have you ever bought a tree from Marder's that's more than 30 feet tall?

Give yourself 25 points.

Does your weekend house have more than 5,000 square feet?

Give yourself 30 points.

Do you buy all your staples at Loaves and Fishes?

Give yourself 30 points.

Do you use your car after midnight to go any place other than home?

Give yourself 20 points.

Are you on a first-name basis with any celebrity?

Give yourself 30 points.

Now, tote up your score. If your total is less than 30, you don't belong here. Forget it, you won't be happy.

If you scored between 30 and 100, you don't really belong here, but you show promise. Try to find a nice rental in Remsenburg and hope that next year you'll do better.

If you scored over 100, you definitely belong here. You're the kind we love to see arrive on Memorial Day and leave on Labor Day.

Now that we've established that, let's talk about where you should rent. Here are some FAQs to help you decide:

Is it true that Southampton means old money and East Hampton means new money?

Yes. If you walk around Southampton, you'll be shocked at how old the money is. You can go shopping on Jobs Lane and get zinc World War II pennies as change. The other day I was on Captain's Neck Lane and saw a gentleman being attacked by blowflies. When I ran to help, I learned that his money had become so old his pants had rotted. The EMTs had to cut out his wallet.

This sort of thing never happens in East Hampton. Much of East Hampton's money has yet to be minted. Last year, East Hampton's Town Board passed an ordinance outlawing cash. "Environmentally unsafe and artistically tacky," they said. If a child wants to open a lemonade stand on Newtown Lane, she has to be willing to take American Express.

In East Hampton, even the panhandlers hate currency. I tried to give fifty cents to a beggar outside the Palm Restaurant, and he said he'd prefer it in frequent flyer miles.

The bottom line is that if you wear green pants, voted for George Bush and are still upset over the disappearance of Herb McCarthy's Bowden Square, you should rent in Southampton. But if you're from Los Angeles, like tanning salons and would never, ever wear socks with your imported loafers, then by all means keep going until you're well past Wainscott.

How old is the money in Westhampton?

Their checks are still in the mail.

Is it true that Southampton attracts older people?

Yes. You may have heard that drug busts have taken place on Hillcrest Avenue in Southampton. What you didn't hear was the nature of the drugs.

I obtained this list from a recent raid by the Southampton Village Police:

12 boxes of out-of-date Metamucil
15 pounds of improperly labeled Centrum Silver
3 vials of illicit Maalox
6 reefers fortified with calcium

In Southampton, you often see summer people coming up from Century Village and cruising the streets looking for action. This can be anything from a game of after-hours shuffleboard to picking up chicks at the VFW Hall.

In East Hampton, you never see such things. In East Hampton, everyone talks Valley Talk.

What about Sag Harbor? Is it really the un-Hampton?

Yes. Because of its lack of pretension, Sag Harbor is the 7-Up of the East End soda fountain. How do we know it's unpretentious? Go to any Sag Harbor event sponsored by Louis Vuitton (profit to the village: $60,000), sit down at one of their sidewalk cafes (profit to the village: $5,000) and cast your eye on all the unpretentious movie stars trying not to be seen. In East Hampton, you have to put up with showboats like Quentin Tarantino. Sag Harbor is so unpretentious, you'll be lucky if you get Wilford Brimley.

What about Noyac?

Noyac is the un-Sag Harbor. Many people who are tired of not being seen in Sag Harbor now prefer not to be seen in Noyac. If in Sag Harbor you're unpretentious, in Noyac you're invisible. But that may change. Word has it that *Architectural Digest* is devoting an entire issue to life in Noyac. It's called "*Where to Park Your Boat—Side Yard or Front?*"

Where's Remsenburg?

Near Liechtenstein.

What do you think of Hampton Bays?

One tries not to. It's so tacky. I mean, a lot of those houses don't even have Wolfe ranges. But if you have no choice, it's probably better than a trailer park, although it really is frightening to think you might have to talk to a neighbor over your back fence.

I'm a Generation X-er who wants to have a really good time, get drunk and have a lot of wild parties. Where do you suggest I look for a house?

Plum Island.

Summer Driving Rules

Now that we've answered your rental questions, let's talk about your driving.

As every year-rounder knows, summer driving in the Hamptons is unlike anything you've ever experienced. Whatever you learned in driver's ed, forget it.

As a convenience for readers, here are some Summer Driving Rules. Let's review them so that on Memorial Day you'll be, as the saying goes, up to speed.

RULE 1. Never signal. Make everyone guess

Starting at the end of May, it is illegal for any driver in the Hamptons to give any other driver the faintest idea of what he's doing. Whether you're turning left, right or coming to a complete stop, inscrutability is the word.

We recommend placing a paper bag over your turn-signal lever to remind you not to use it. The only exception is when you're leaving the Hamptons and taking the Long Island Expressway back to New York. Then, you should put on your turn signal at Exit 70 and not turn it off until you've reached the city.

In the same vein, when making a turn, use only accepted summer procedures. In the Hamptons, these are: Starting a mile away, slow down and creep at ten miles per hour so that no one knows what's going to happen. Keep creeping, until suddenly, when least expected, you veer quickly and erratically across opposing lanes. Starting on Memorial Day, anyone seen making a prudent turn will be made to enroll in AARP.

RULE 2. Never enter an intersection without creating a hazard, confusion and inconvenience

Starting on Memorial Day, the proper way to enter an intersection is as follows:

1. Approach slowly. 2. Come to a complete stop. 3. Wait until there is approaching traffic. 4. At the last moment, pull in front of the traffic and drive at a snail's pace so that others can leisurely read your bumper stickers. Keep driving at this pace until someone tries to pass you, at which point speed up and give him the finger.

RULE 3. Keep to your side of the road unless there is opposing traffic, in which case, keep to theirs

Southampton being the oldest English settlement in New York, many consider it appropriate to do things the way King George would have done them. That means driving on the left.

As many of you local pick-up truck dudes know, the best way is to drive on *both* sides of the road, with your wheels straddling the yellow line. This is particularly effective on narrow back roads, where there are thrills and chills around every bend.

RULE 4. Make U-turns often and unpredictably

There are two ways to make a Hamptons U-turn:

1. Wait until you've reached a four-way intersection, then do a quick 180, disrupting traffic in all directions.

2. Choose the narrowest part of the road, then cut a swath across someone's lawn.

No matter which way you choose, be sure to complete your maneuver by making an appropriate obscene gesture, so that everyone will know you're having fun.

RULE 5. On Route 27, always drive faster than the cars ahead of you, but slower than those behind

This takes skill, but experienced summer drivers know that if you enter the highway and there's no one behind you, you should gun your car until you've caught up with the car ahead, then breathe down that car's tailpipe for the next five miles.

Conversely, if you enter the highway and the only cars are behind you (hopefully because you've cut them off, as explained in Rule 2), continue driving at a snail's pace until the traffic is backed up for several miles. This is particularly fun on Saturday evenings when everyone's trying to make a movie.

RULE 6. In the villages and hamlets, ignore all direction arrows and yield-to-pedestrians signs. They're for locals and are a mark of low status

Everyone knows that turn arrows are for rubes, so if you're in a Mercedes, Porsche or Land Rover, ignore them. You're too important.

Similarly, pay no attention to those quaint "Ped Xing" signs. Who knows what they mean. The only people who obey them are little old ladies in Oldsmobiles.

RULE 7. When parking, never park between the lines. Try to take up as many spaces as possible

If it's a parallel parking zone, park diagonally. If it's a diagonal parking zone, park parallel. Always make sure your car takes up at least two spaces and is three or more feet from the curb.

Last but not least, try to remember that the object of summer driving in the Hamptons is to be as annoying as you can, without harming your own paint-job. If everyone follows these few simple rules, this summer should be as enjoyable as the last.

Choosing a Hamptons Car

It is very important to have the right car, and I don't think I need to tell you that is not a Buick. You're not a potato farmer.

A Mercedes, BMW or Audi will suffice, but it's better to be on the safe side and have a Porsche, Maserati or Lamborghini. After all, parking valets have feelings too.

My favorite Hamptons car is the Hummer. Yes, it's now defunct, but it still occupies a warm spot in the Hamptons' heart. As a former English major, I took it upon myself to pay poetic tribute to this four-wheeled marvel. With a tip of the hat to William Blake, here's an ode to:

The Hummer

Hummer! Hummer! burning gas
As with tinted glass you pass,
What demented hand or brow
Could frame a fearful box like thou?

SUV so wide and fat,
Did Ira Rennert* make you that,
Or did you too much grease consume
To make you go "Var-room! Var-room!"?

Or were you somehow supersized
On Big Macs, Cokes and starchy fries,
Or is it just an ego thing
That makes you automotive's bling?

You must not care a fig or hoot
That while you swell the Saudis' loot
The soldiers in the real Humvees
Are getting killed in twos and threes

Or that while you on cell phone yak
You're being scorned behind your back
By those who think your clumsy hulk
Is short on style and long on bulk.

What spews like muck from your exhaust
Will deem the earth's best causes lost,
And drain what's left of mankind's oil
While you both skies and seas despoil.

---

*See note, page 24

I think of this most everyday
As when I leave a parking bay
And try to see around your rear
And can't tell if the coast is clear

Or when I see you bearing down
Astride the highway's center crown,
Which makes the smaller cars take flight
By swerving to the left and right.

It makes me contemplate just who
Would want to own a car like you,
Unless of course it's to announce
That he's the only one who counts.

Hummer! Hummer! burning gas
As with tinted glass you pass,
What demented hand or brow
Dared frame a noxious thing like thou?

Land Preservation

One of the ongoing struggles on the East End is land preservation. That's because this is a skinny little spit on a skinny little island and the amount of available land is very finite. This is something that is often lost on our politicians.

In lean times the developer always seems to get his way because he argues that the locals need jobs, which is true. But in flush times he gets his way too, because he's got all the money.

This makes it very frustrating to the people who have moved out here thinking that the McMansions they built would be the last. There always seems to be room for more.*

To some extent, this trend has been curbed by what is called the Community Preservation Fund—a fund supported by a transfer tax any time a piece of property changes hands. But it's still a tough battle and in the end the developer always seems to get his way.

Fortunately, I have come up with a remedy. That's what newspaper columnists are for. They're supposed to look at intractable problems and come up with remedies. That's what earns us the big bucks.

My remedy is that we should secede from Suffolk County, then declare ourselves a national park. Here's how it would work:

The entire East End would become frozen in time. Think of it like Pompeii or as a kind of seaside Williamsburg, with Lexuses. There would be no more fields sold, no more homes built, no more drugstores merged. All the developers would have to pack up and go home, and all the people in the construction industry would have to undergo job training so that they can be re-employed as—yes—park rangers.

This park, which I propose to call Peconic Hampton National Monument, would be one of the largest preservations on the East Coast. It would stretch from Westhampton to Montauk, and you would not be able to build so much as a dog house here. People would come from all over the world and say, "So these were the

---

*An example of this paradox was when a former Southampton Town Supervisor pushed tirelessly for more homebuilding throughout his administration, then complained bitterly when the buyers of those homes did not want the cell phone towers he was selling in their backyards. "The ingratitude!" he said.

Fabulous Hamptons back in the day! Aren't we lucky to have them forever preserved for posterity!"

I propose that a hundred years from now our citizens should be dressed just as they are today, so that visiting Chinese, disembarking from the same pokey Cannonball Express weekenders disembark from now, can have them pose for snapshots.

"You Yuppie?" they'll say. "Talk Yuppie please!"

There would be no new cars or trucks. All the vehicles would be just as they are now, meticulously preserved to the last detail. On Sunday afternoons, the Chinese would board the Cannonball and head back west seeing BMWs and Mercedes caught in the same mess they're caught in today. The Chinese could point their cameras out the window and capture a perfect re-enactment of a Hamptons traffic snarl.

I want a man dressed like a potato farmer to stand on the corner of Main Street and Job's Lane so that visiting school children can approach and ask what he's got in his hand. When he tells them it's a potato, they'll say, "Oooh! We thought they came off French fry trees!"

In my Peconic Hampton National Monument there would be plenty of work and no room for slackers. It's hard keeping a national monument clean, so there would be no end of lawn mowing, hedge trimming and kudzu-pulling. Visitors would be able to go to a perfectly preserved North Sea Landfill and see what it was like during The Great Hamptons Garbage Crisis. "And this is where they dumped their old Ralph Lauren and Eddie Bauer cast-offs," a ranger in a Smokey the Bear hat would tell them. "That mountain over there is full of soiled Laura Ashley prints."

Some of the Chinese might wonder why there aren't silversmiths working in Mr. Pelletreau's shop or whalers setting out from Sag Harbor. Our construction-workers-turned-park-rangers would explain that by the 1990's the only Hamptons industries were t-shirts, fudge-making, and single-person networking. "If you want some fun," they'll say, "go to Bobby Van's tonight and watch our locals re-enact a genuine hook-up. There'll be waiters in khaki, Duckwalk chardonnay, and professionals exchanging business cards just like a hundred years ago."

There would be nothing fake about this park. We'd feature real waves rolling off real seas creating real erosion. "You want special effects, go to MGM," the rangers will explain. "Even Steven Spielberg had to fight off real deer here."

We'd take our visitors for a drive to Sagaponack, where they'd see the remains of one of the original Seven Wonders of the World—the Ira Rennert Mausoleum.* This massive pile would stand just as it does today—a memorial to the great man who gave us the Hummer and a horde of air-polluting industries. "Ah so!" our awe-struck visitors will say. "Better than our Great Wall or the Pyramid of Cheops!"

Our visitors would want to know how many slaves lost their lives putting up that monstrosity, and the rangers will say, "None, although we did almost lose several politicians."

I tell you, this park will be the answer to all our problems. It's the only way to keep our tradesmen busy and The Nature Con-

---

*The story of this Uber-citiot and his house is one of the great legends of the East End. Using various front names, Rennert, an early junk bond salesman who became rich buying up high-polluting industries and companies like Am General, makers of the Humvee and the Hummer, procured 63 acres of oceanfront property in Sagaponack and put up a 66,000-square-foot house with 29 bedrooms, 39 baths, a basketball court, bowling alley, and, well, you name it. It became a kind of Battle of the Millionaires as his wealthy neighbors tried in vain to stop him. The house was perhaps best described by a British friend of mine, who, when he saw it, said, "That's not a house, it's a CIA operation." But at least Rennert, who was awarded The Awful Truth Man of the Year Award in 1999 by filmmaker Michael Moore, disproves the myth that all the obnoxious money in Southampton is WASP. Jerkiness is a game anyone can play.

servancy happy. To cap it all off, imagine how wonderful it will be when, at the close of day, all the tourists line up with their cameras on Lily Pond Lane to see one of Nature's most dazzling water shows.

There, every hour on the hour, like clockwork, there will be a long, low grumble, a hiss of escaping steam, and then the sight of geysers shooting majestically into the air.

"*Ah so!*" the Chinese will squeal with delight, and we would tell them, "Yes, you can set your clocks by those estate section sprinkler systems."

The Hamptons County Fair

If the movement to secede from Suffolk County succeeds, it will mean a lot of changes. Our new county, which would be called Peconic County*, will have to have a county courthouse, a county medical examiner and a county executive.

We will also need a county fair, so a few years ago I assembled a group of notable East End tastemakers and asked for their thinking on the subject. Some of them are gone now, but their opinions live on. Here's how it went:

Martha Stewart: I think we all agree that the Peconic County Fair should be unique to our area. No apple pies, no 4-H hog growers. Things like that are so. . .well, so upstate, aren't they?

---

*There has actually been such a proposal. It has been floated for some years by Fred Thiele, our state assemblyman. The problem is, the county legislature is not too keen on it—they would lose all that nice East End tax revenue—and Albany is not too keen on it either, since it would encourage places like Staten Island to pursue their own secession dreams. Still, many people think it's a worthy cause.

Ralph Lauren: I agree. We mustn't be tacky. We need a fair that reflects our East End lifestyle.

Charlotte Ford: And by that, I assume, we do mean the Hamptons.

Ralph Lauren: Well, we certainly don't mean Riverhead, do we?

Donna Karan : I think it should be very south-of-the-highway.* Something we'd be proud to take our friends to.

Martha Stewart: I suppose our first problem is where to hold it.

Charlotte Ford: Place is everything.

George Plimpton: I'd be glad to have it at my house. I've got a few spare hectares lying around.

Martha Stewart: That's very generous of you, George.

Ronald Perelman: And, if I do say so, an ideal tax shelter!

George Plimpton: We could get the Grucci Brothers to bring in cherry bombs.

Charlotte Ford: Oh, George, not again!

George Plimpton: Well, I like fireworks! We could hold a contest to see who could set off the biggest detonator.

Charlotte Ford: George, do try to control yourself.

Calvin Klein: What other events should we have?

Martha Stewart: Well, I don't think we want Midwestern tractor pulls, do we?

Charlotte Ford: No, they're so *outre*.

Donna Karan: And, I suspect, air-polluting.

---

*This is a popular Hamptons term. It derives from the fact that, in the old days, all of the better houses were south of the Montauk Highway, nearer the ocean, and the commoners all lived north of the highway, nearer the sand pits. That is no longer the case. Since Wall Street began handing out billion-dollar bonuses like Christmas turkeys, now there are plenty of showcase houses north of the highway, too. I myself live north of the highway, although, as will be explained later, my house is a drag on the market.

Brooke Astor: I've never seen a tractor I'd want to drive to a dinner party.

Jerry Della Femina: If I may speak.

Martha Stewart: You always do, Jerry.

Jerry Della Femina: I think we might want to have a 4-wheel Land Rover pull. We'll get these Land Rovers, see, tie their bumpers together and the one that remains intact wins a Rolex.

Martha Stewart: *Love* it! *Love* it!

Ralph Lauren: Just one suggestion. Let me pick out what material we tie the bumpers with. Nothing synthetic. I've got some marvelous tartan remnants. . .

Elaine K. G. Benson: What about food?

Martha Stewart: What about it, Elaine K. G.?

Elaine K. G. Benson: I'm under the impression these fairs have food. I saw a movie with Ann-Margret once, and she went to a fair where food was served. Baking contests, things like that.

George Plimpton: Well, we certainly don't want pies and cakes!

Jerry Della Femina: Absolutely not. That is so up-island!

George Plimpton: I think we need recipes that reflect how we live out here. Cutting-edge stuff. Bake-offs with attitude.

Martha Stewart: I happen to have made a list based on some of the books I've written. For openers, I suggest a nice mesclun salad contest. We'll get some fresh greens from the Green Thumb and award a prize for the most interesting vinaigrette.

Charlotte Ford: That does sound yum!

Brooke Astor: And so non-fattening!

Martha Stewart: And we could pass out ribbons for haricots verts gardening. The gardener who grows the thinnest bean would win a portobello mushroom and a jar of chipotle sauce.

Jerry Della Femina: We could have it judged by one of my restaurant chefs.

Calvin Klein: Say, this could be better than a designer showcase house!

Martha Stewart: And for livestock, we could have a Jack Russell barking contest. The one that barks longest gets a Paloma Picasso dog collar.

Elaine K. G. Benson: I have a feeling we're omitting the children. What about the children?

Martha Stewart: I've heard of them. What about them?

Elaine K. G. Benson: We don't want any of those corny 4-H Clubs. But there ought to be something the little waifs can participate in.

At this point, there was a long and awkward silence. Ron Perelman got up and cell-phoned his broker. Ralph made an appointment at his tanning salon. As usual, it was Martha who saved the day.

Martha Stewart: I know! Let's invite the kids to a Biggest Pet Clam Contest!

The Champ, And Still Going

Are the Hamptons Prejudiced?

You may wonder if there's any prejudice on the East End. After all, there is, as I said, a lot of old money out here, and old-money can be snooty.

So the answer is, yes, there is some prejudice, but if you're rich enough, who cares?

For instance, when a bunch of billionaires were denied membership in some of our local golf clubs because they were Jewish, did they sit around and whine? They did not. They just went out and built their own golf club. They called it The Atlantic and made it just as snobbish as the gentile clubs.

The Atlantic has a very nice course, and the fact that none of its members know how to play golf has been no impediment whatsoever. They just hired a top-of-the-line pro, and now they're swinging with the best of them.*

But about this prejudice. A few years ago, one of our town supervisors said that he was opposed to a proposal to create a "Latino advisory board" on the grounds that, as an Italian-American, he had been the victim of ethnic prejudice himself and didn't see why the Latinos should get any more consideration than he had gotten. The fact that every day rednecks from up-island stop by and shout epithets at the Latino day laborers was no big deal. The supervisor had survived, so why shouldn't they?

---

*Although their solution was downright chintzy compared with that of another multimillionaire who was denied membership in The Atlantic. He just bought a bunch of land across the street from The Atlantic and put in his own private course. There's more than one way to thumb your nose at the hoi polloi.

Frankly, I was shocked to read that our supervisor had been the victim of prejudice, so I decided to investigate.

First, I went to the pro shop at Shinnecock Hills Golf Club. I figured this was as good a place as any to find a scientific cross-section of our populace.

Sure enough, there was every kind of blue-eyed white man you could imagine, some in plaid pants and some in pants with ducks on them. It was a real melting pot.

I put the question to them bluntly: "Do you think Italian-Americans are being discriminated against on the East End?" I stood poised with notebook, ready to record their answers.

I am happy to report that, to a man, every one of those Shinnecock Hills members answered: "Balderdash!"

Balderdash is a word you often hear at Shinnecock Hills. Whenever someone slices a ball or misses a putt, you'll hear him cry, "Balderdash!" It's the old WASP equivalent of the word Italian-Americans use when they want to sound like Tony Soprano. When you hear Tony Soprano, what he's really saying is the Italian-American version of "balderdash."

At Shinnecock Hills, when you roam around the links, you hear a withering barrage of balderdashes, pshaws, fudges, fiddlesticks and tommyrots. You also hear the occasional poppycock. That's because the Shinnecocks and the Poppycocks are ancient rivals and often use each others' names in vain.

A completely unbiased survey of Shinnecock Hills (as well as Poppycock Hills) revealed that there is absolutely no evidence of prejudice against Italian-Americans, and in fact anyone not of Anglo-Saxon extraction can feel free to caddy there any time.

The supervisor, I learned, is also welcome at the Maidstone Country Club in East Hampton. I talked to the chef there, and he said Wednesday night is Prince Spaghetti Night. The supervisor can stop by the kitchen any Wednesday and trade marinara recipes.

But I wasn't willing just to take these WASPs' word for it. I wanted to hear from someone a little "closer to the quick." So I called Bob DeLuca, president of what was then Group for the South Fork but is now Group for the East End. Bob had been very critical of our supervisor's environmental policies and on occasion had been known to think that the man was off his rocker.

I said, "Bob, is it possible that what really bothers you about our supervisor is that he's Italian-American?"

Mr. DeLuca thought about that a minute, then consulted with Steve Biasetti, their environmental expert. I could hear Dean Martin songs playing in the background.

A couple of minutes latter, Mr. DeLuca got back on the phone and gave me his answer. It was the Italian-American version of "balderdash."

Next, I went to Buckley's Pub. I figured who should know better about the problems of ethnic conflict than the people who hang out in a place covered with shamrocks?

But when I asked the customers there if they had ever witnessed any prejudice against Italian-Americans, they swore they hadn't. "As long as he hates the Brits and won't let the gays march in his Columbus Day parade," they said, "he can drink all the Guinness here he wants."

Finally, I decided to go to the Shinnecocks themselves. Mind you, the Shinnecocks are very sensitive and one has to be careful how one approaches them. You can't just throw the word Shinnecock around like you can Italian-American. (I once wrote a column suggesting that the Shinnecocks have no sense of humor, and the next week a letter to the editor appeared saying that they have a great sense of humor, but no one had said anything funny yet.)

With that as proviso, I am happy to report that the Shinnecocks agree with the Buckley's crowd, Group for the South Fork and the country club WASPs. They swore that there is absolutely no animosity toward Italian-Americans or any other group on the East End, and anyone who says otherwise is a dirty Poppycock.

The Latino Issue

I mentioned that we have a certain Latino issue out here. That's because Latinos do a major share of the work on the East End, and some people hate that. Of course they don't have any interest in doing the work themselves, but they don't want Latinos doing it because, well, Latinos talk funny. That means that if anything goes wrong, it must be the Latinos' fault.

Incredibly, a fragment from a hitherto-unknown episode of *Star Trek* has turned up in Southampton's Rogers Memorial Library bearing light on this issue. Called *The Aliens*, it goes like this:

> The Starship Enterprise is in trouble. The crew is running out of food and must find a hospitable planet upon which to land.
>
> Captain Kirk consults Chekov, their navigator, who says that their best bet is 7-Eleven, a small planet just a few light years away. "It's like Earth," he says, "only more so."
>
> "There's a problem," says Mr. Spock, consulting his *Hitchhiker's Guide to the Galaxy*. "It's populated by people who came from other planets but have since grown hostile to aliens. It may not be safe to land."

Kirk says they have no choice—it's either that or starve—so Scotty beams Kirk and Mr. Spock down to assess of the situation.

On 7-Eleven, they find themselves in a parking lot next to a convenience store. "Perhaps if we offer our services," says Spock, "they'll give us food."

The first person they approach says he'll be glad to help and piles them into the back of a pickup truck. He hauls them off to a job cleaning toilets and cutting grass. It's horrible work.

After a 14-hour day, they ask if they can be paid. "What?" the man says. "You aren't even legal and you want to be paid? You look funny and one of you has pointy ears. Scram, or I'll call the cops!"

They go back to the convenience store, where a second person says he'll give them work if they can show him a green card.

"What's a green card?" asks the captain.

"It's a card that says you're allowed to be here," says the man.

"Do you have such a card?" says the captain.

At that the man becomes abusive. "How dare you insult an honest 7-Elevenian!" he cries. "I've got a good mind to turn you over to Interplanetary Immigration!"

A woman at a tire store takes pity on them and offers them soup and bread. "I don't care where you're from," she says. "I can't stand seeing living creatures starve."

The space travelers are grateful, but soon Code Enforcement arrives.

"These men aren't allowed to eat unless they're legal," says the officer. "Your soup is in defiance of 7-Eleven's ordinances. You either turn off your hotplate, or I'll throw you in jail."

By now an angry crowd has gathered. Spock tells them, "Please! We aren't here to hurt you. We only want what your ancestors wanted—a better life and a fuller stomach."

> "Bah!" cries the crowd. "Our ancestors were fine people who came here legally! They would never have taken away our toilet-cleaning jobs! You two must be sex perverts, running around like that in your long underwear!"
>
> "With all due respect," says Mr. Spock, "most of your ancestors did not come here legally or illegally. Until 88 years ago, you hardly had any laws at all. It was only then that you decided to keep certain people out because you didn't like them. But many of your ancestors were equally despised, and it took them years to assimilate."
>
> "Spoken like the filthy Vulcan you are!" cries a man, and a chant arises, "Kill them! Kill them!"
>
> Spock turns to Captain Kirk. "You see, Captain, it's as I feared. They are a bunch of bigoted, inhumane louts who have no sense of their own history. They'll blame us for everything that goes wrong. If they lose their homes, they'll blame us. If their hospital costs go up, they'll blame us. We cannot in good conscience ask our crew to come down here and risk their lives. I suggest that we have Scotty beam us back up so that we can leave and find a more hospitable planet."
>
> "Ah, 'beam us back up'!" cries a heckler who's been walking around with a placard that says, "They broke the law when they defied gravity!" "You come here and frighten our women, litter our streets, then you go back to your fancy spaceship and leave us to clean up the mess! Hanging's too good for you!"

At that the episode ends, perhaps because the show's creator couldn't figure out how to resolve the situation, or perhaps because the network got cold feet. Whatever, the following week the series was canceled and replaced by a show starring Lou Dobbs as an implacable detective on the trail of the Cisco Kid. It was called "El Fugitivo" and was a huge success.

Blackhampton

Here might be a good place to talk seriously about one of the least visible and least discussed minorities on the East End—African-Americans. Yes, there is a black populace on the East End, but their voices are rarely heard. They are clustered in places like Riverside/Flanders, Hillcrest Avenue and David Whites Lane in Southampton and along the turnpike in Bridgehampton. Many are well-established families whose lineage predates that of most white families. They came here years ago to work on farms and to help salvage wrecked ships, and here they have stayed.

It is often noted that many of our Shinnecocks are almost indistinguishable from African-Americans. That makes sense. Since both groups were excluded from white society, they naturally commingled. If nothing else, they had their outsider status in common.

A few years ago, I decided to investigate one of the most problematical public schools on the East End, the black-dominated K-through-12 school in Bridgehampton. As a newcomer, I was puzzled by the fact that this school was spending more money per capita on its students than any other school, yet it remained one of the state's poorest-performing schools. All I knew about it was that it was heavily minority and had an outstanding basketball legacy.

What I found was surprising—and not at all stereotypical of underperforming schools. First of all, Bridgehampton School's physical plant is beautiful, with tile floors and state-of-the-art classrooms. Once you get past the garish yellow sign out front that looks like an A&W Root Beer sign, you find yourself in a very pleasant surrounding.

Next, you notice that the children seem happy and well-mannered. Discipline has never been a problem at the Bridgehampton School, and many parents—particularly those of children with special needs—think the school is wonderful.

The student body used to be predominantly black, but now it is about equally divided between blacks, whites and Hispanics. When I visited, I was told that the recent influx of Hispanic students was causing some tension. Not only were the Hispanics the new kids on the block, but because some of the black kids' parents thought the Hispanic parents were taking their jobs away, the black kids were reflecting what they heard at home.

Still, these problems never seemed to amount to much more than you'd find in any suburban school, and there was no sign of gang violence or widespread drug use (at least not that I saw).

So why does Bridgehampton rate so low in achievement?

The first problem is size. Here you might think that we're talking about crowded classrooms and a poor teacher-student ratio, but we're talking about the opposite. Those who claim to know a bit about education explained that the Bridgehampton School is simply too small.

In any given year, the school's enrollment is likely to be no more than 150 students—and that's for kindergarten through twelfth grade. For the younger students, this is fine. In the lower grades, there may be ten or 11 kids in a class, and everyone gets along. But as the kids grow older, there are the usual rivalries and cliques, and this is when white parents are most likely to take their children out and put them in another school.

This leaves a hard core of minority students who lack the proper motivation or home environment. The parents never went to college, so see no reason why their children should.

Elsewhere in this book, I mention a Bridgehampton resident named Dennis Suskind. Dennis Suskind is a former Goldman Sachs executive who at one point thought it might be nice to mentor some of these poor kids and show them the opportunities they were missing. As he described it to me, although upon graduation most of these kids could receive scholarships and loans to a range of good universities, few were motivated to try. He would urge them day after day to fill out their college applications, and they would refuse. After a year or two, he gave up.

My guide to this misunderstood world—my Beatrice, if you will—was a black woman named Jackie Pool. At the time, Jackie was working in a program that introduced reading and educational play into minority students' homes. Jackie told me that the thing I must understand is that, poor as the school might be, the blacks along the turnpike view it as their private institution and don't want anyone to change it. The parents have a handle on their kids' behavior at the school and are afraid that if the school closes they will lose an intimate link to their children's lives.

When I finished my investigation, I wrote a series of columns about it, and one day I received an unsigned e-mail from a student who said that when she started reading my columns she was afraid I was going to say all the bad things white people always say about her school. But by the time she had finished the series, she felt that I had been reasonably fair. I think she was giving me a B-.

Before we leave this subject, I should explain that not all black communities on the East End are underprivileged. For instance, there are several communities that have welcomed successful blacks for years. As you drive through communities like Ninevah, Eastville and Azurest, for instance, you will see lovely, well-kept houses with neat yards, pruned shrubs and all the accoutrements of an upper-middleclass neighborhood. In the old pre-civil-rights days, if someone like Duke Ellington or Cab Calloway wanted to get away from it all, this is where he could come.* Such communities still exist, and are as idyllic as ever.

Power Brokering in the Hamptons

Those in the know realize that when it comes to real power broking on the East End, you don't go to Nello or the Maidstone Arms. The real action takes place in the morning at a little retro establishment in Bridgehampton called the Candy Kitchen.

There are several such places in the Hamptons, but none quite like the Candy Kitchen. In Southampton, there's a place called Sip 'n' Soda, which in décor and atmosphere rivals the Candy Kitchen (both look as if they should still have Connie Francis songs in their jukeboxes), but it doesn't draw from the celebrity crowd that lives in Sagaponack and East Hampton.

I was sitting in the Candy Kitchen one day when a man in a white suit came up and asked if I was the famous *Southampton Press* columnist.

"I am," I said. "Who are you?"

"Tom Wolfe," he said. "I write, too."

I was not familiar with his work but, being generous, I invited him to sit.

I was about to give him some writerly advice—"Make sure your verbs agree with your nouns, Tom"—when a woman

*There's a joke among African-Americans that these places aren't East Hampton or Southampton. They're Lionel Hampton.

stepped off the Jitney and said if I ever wanted anything, all I had to do was whistle. "You do know how to whistle, don't you?" she asked.

I asked who she was, and she said her name was Lauren, but Bogey had always called her Baby.

Baby, Tom and I chatted awhile, and I was about to share some scrapple and grits with them when Billy Joel came in and asked if I'd like to do some haul-seining with him. "Love to," I said, "but as you can see, I'm eating. Tom here's a writer. Baby's a Jitney worker."

Billy said he was pleased to meet them, and as he reached for a flapjack I heard someone say he didn't know who the guy with the fish net was, but the bloke beside him was Reynolds Dodson, the famous *Southampton Press* columnist.

"Hey, Alec," I said, recognizing the voice as that of yet another hopeful actor who is always trying to worm a plug out of me. "Why don't you come over and take a load off? This here's Tom, and this is Billy the Haul-Seiner."

Alec said he was glad to have a chance to sit down with some just plain folks for a change, and asked if we had room for his friend, Kim.* "Sure," I said, "bring her over. Baby here can make her a Jitney driver."

---

*I date myself here. Soon after this meeting Alec and Kim started their own Punch and Judy Show and the world was treated to the second-most unseemly divorce spectacle ever to arise out of the East End. The most unseemly, of course, was the one between Christie Brinkley and her philandering husband, Peter Cook. Cook had been discovered having an affair with his 18-year-old assistant while also spending inordinate amounts of time visiting pornographic websites. This resulted in one of the wildest divorce trials ever to delight Page Six. (Even Christie's ex, Billy Joel, got involved.) But Alec and Kim run a close second, making you wonder whether there's something in the water out here that makes marriages dissolve on contact.

"Don't look now," said Billy, "but I think that's Barry Diller and his ne'er-do-well pal Ron Perelman over there. I'll bet they'll come over and try to social-climb."

"Yeah, they'll be hoping Reynolds can give them some tips on career advancement," said Kim. "People are like that. They'll use you and use you, Reynolds."

A guy with a cigar came by and introduced himself as Ben Gazarra, a trouper who had done some TV work back in the seventies. "Sit down," I said. "This is Tom the Pencil-Pusher."

"Any friend of Reynolds' is a friend of mine," said Ben, and as he sat down he knocked ashes all over the Jitney lady's lap.

"Actually," I said, "I'd love to go haul-seining with you, Billy, but I promised Jerry Della Femina I'd come out to East Hampton and help him set up his farm stand. Jerry's doing his bit for the farmers, you know, just as you are for the fishermen."

"That's what I've always liked about you, Reynolds," said Billy. "You've never lost touch with the little people."

"Speaking of which," I said, "don't look now, but there's another out-of-work actor coming through the door. Maybe you ought to meet him, Ben. He was all the rage in the pre-MTV era."

Alan Alda came over, and I told him he and Ben ought to get together and work out a little idea I had for a pilot about a Korean War Army doctor who's diagnosed with a fatal illness and spends the next five years running from story to story.

"I like it," said Alan.

"Me, too," said Ben, and the next thing I knew they were exchanging business cards.

Stefanie Powers stopped by wanting some advice on horse farming, then Sally Quinn popped in and said she had been sent over by her husband, who needed some help getting ahead in the newspaper business. "Sal," I said, "I'll give you a raincheck. I promised Ed Albee I'd read a new play he's been working on."

Steve Spielberg wanted to know if I could mention a new project he was developing in my column, then Marv Hamlisch passed by and hummed a few bars of something I didn't recognize. The next thing I knew it was almost two in the afternoon—time to pack up and head out to Jerry's place. As I left, I saw Ron Perelman smiling at Baby and trying to give her the eye. It probably wouldn't go anywhere, but I'd do what I could for them.

The Deer Problem: Solution # 1

Deer are a serious problem in the Hamptons. There are far more deer now than when the first settlers landed, and they don't seem to be the least deterred by human beings. They've just changed their diet from grass to hosta.

Nowhere has the problem been worse than in North Haven, where a few years ago the citizenry almost came to blows over the subject. (The rancor even made a segment on *60 Minutes*.)

On one side of the debate were the people who wanted to save what little was left of their gardens and on the other side was a group of Deer Ladies who had grown up watching *Bambi*.

At the time, I noted that one side's argument could be summed up as "shoot the buggers," while the other favored contraception.

I happened to agree with the latter. I thought contraceptives were by far the more humane approach, but one thing troubled me. How could we be sure the deer would use them?

Don't laugh. It's well known that deer are becoming more like us everyday. At the time I wrote this, a doe had just been found floundering around Fort Tryon Park in Manhattan. No city official would confirm it, but I suspected she was looking for Bloomingdale's.

It's all well and good to say that deer are intelligent animals capable of deciding their own destinies (*Bucks Are From Mars, Does Are From Venus,* etc.), but since they've been hanging around with us so much, it's possible that they've lost the gift.

I know for a fact that you can put a contraceptive machine in every men's room in the country and a lot of guys won't use them. Why? Because we're good-time Charlies, that's why. We may know in our hearts that we're as guilty of overpopulating the planet as women are, but there's this little voice inside us that says, "Oh, what the heck, let her take care of it."

I think it's very likely that you could put contraceptive machines on every tree in North Haven, and the bucks would simply walk right past them. As for getting them to buy them at drugstores—hey, they're bashful enough without laying that on them.

Of course in many cases substance abuse may be involved. You get a bunch of deer standing around drinking and licking salt at 3 a.m., there's really no telling where things will lead.

Even sober, male deer can be duty-shirkers. Some of them would probably complain that contraceptives are "unnatural." Others would say they cut down on "spontaneity" and put the female in an offish mood. (I tried to ask some does about this, but they got so embarrassed, they jumped three fences in an attempt to get away.)

However you cut it, I think it's going to take a lot of sex education to get the bucks to use those things, and we all know the antagonism *that* will arouse.

In the past, I would have said that females are the better bet, but now I'm not so sure. Single-motherhood has become so lion-

Irresponsible Buck at 3 a.m.

ized, I think that if you got a bunch of female deer together they'd sound like guests on Sally Jessy Raphael.

Little attention is paid to the fawns. Male fawns particularly need bucks to teach them how to rub antlers and butt their heads together. Without such role models, they'll just go out and crash into cars. But today's females don't seem to care. They feel that relations with bucks are so strained, they're within their rights to raise fawns on her own, with or without Pat Robertson's approval.

I have heard that there are elements within the Republican party which favor cutting off all aid to North Haven if it pursues a policy of enforced contraception. They want the village to control deer the way Dick Cheney would —with an AK-47. In my opinion, that's wrong. I think we have to give the deer freedom of choice and hope they'll learn to act responsibly.

No, the rational way is contraceptives. Give the does pills and a pocket calendar. Try to teach the bucks to use the condoms. Save the AK-47s for our teenagers.

The Deer Problem: Solution # 2

It has occurred to me that there's another answer to the deer problem, and it would also solve our Circus Problem.

You didn't know we had a Circus Problem? Well, we do.

One of the annual skirmishes to which East Enders are subjected is the rabid attack by animal lovers on the Clyde Beatty-Cole Brothers Circus, which is sponsored by the Southampton Elks Club. Every year, the Clyde Beatty-Cole Brothers Circus comes to town and every year they are accused of—well, bestiality. There is a group that believes that the circus mistreats its animals, and they want it outlawed.

I have a solution. Let's invite the Clyde Beatty-Cole Brothers Circus to come out here and abuse their animals as usual, then let's take the animals to North Haven and set them loose on the deer.

Doesn't that make sense? As the newly freed lions run through people's back yards tearing the frightened deer to pieces, we could pride ourselves on our eco-morality and the marvelous way we're allowing Nature to run its course. Yes, the fur would lie thicker than the kudzu on Route 114, but the anti-circus people would be appeased and the North Havenites could reclaim their shrubbery.

I called the Clyde Beatty-Cole Brothers Circus and asked what they thought of this, and to my surprise they didn't like it. They said their animals were valuable and they didn't want them running around where Deer Ladies might yell at them. I pointed out that their circus would never find peace as long as the animals were in cages and the Deer Ladies weren't, but they said they had tried putting the Deer Ladies in cages and no one wanted to see them.

I'll admit, there are drawbacks to my plan. For instance, it might be hard to get the lions to concentrate on deer when there are so many humans around. "Why," a rational lion might ask, "should I chase something as fast as a deer when there are so many easier meals wearing flip-flops on Long Wharf?"

Drawback to Deer Solution #2

On the other hand, they might go after the Deer Ladies, which would make everyone happy. As North Havenites watched those troublesome women run screaming for their lives among the half-eaten cotoneasters, they could cast their vote with either a thumbs-up or thumbs-down, the way Romans did in the Coliseum.

Anyway, I think it's a good idea, and tonight, as you hear the Long Island Rail Road wailing its forlorn way toward wherever it goes out there in Montauk, you can rest assured that I'll be lying awake, trying to refine the details.

The Long Island Rail Road

One of the great assets of our community is the Long Island Railroad. Several times a day it carries a handful of city people to this fabulous playground at speeds approaching those of an ox cart. And the amazing thing is, the more streamlined the trains get, the slower they go. It's called the LIRR Paradox.

Lately, there's been talk about the railroad's train whistles. Apparently they changed the pitch or something, and people have complained.

Naturally, I looked into the matter, and what I discovered was that the train whistles weren't attached to trains. After 11 p.m., what you're hearing is just the whistle, not the train, that being one of many budgetary measures the railroad incorporated during the 1980s.

I found this out by chance. As an insomniac, I have long wondered about the train whistles I hear at 1:30 and 3:30 a.m. every morning. I've said to myself, "Here's a railroad no one rides, yet it's going to and from Montauk all night. Who's on it?"

Intrepid reporter that I am, I tracked down a Long Island Rail Road official at a secret phone number they keep for live communications between humans. The railroad has very few such numbers. Not wanting to hear from the public, they only list numbers that have computers at the other end. And whistles are not on the automated phone menu.

But I obtained this number and got a startled woman who had apparently not talked to a live person in 25 years.

"How did you get this number?" she asked.

"Never mind," I said. "What I want to know is, who's riding all those trains whose whistles are keeping me awake at night?"

There was a long and pregnant pause. I'm not saying the woman was pregnant, but her pause was. When she recovered, she said, "No one."

I said, "*No one?*"

"If you must know," she said, "the railroad discontinued nightly train service back in 1988. The whistles you hear have been pre-recorded and played from a steam cart that goes back and forth between Montauk and Speonk four times a night after 11 p.m."

She said that the railroad had taken a poll and learned that the only thing people liked about it was its whistle. "It came in third on a list of favorite Long Island sounds," she said, "behind geese honking and Billy Joel's *Uptown Girl*. We realized that it was silly spending so much money on train service when all anyone wanted was the whistle, so we just recorded the whistle, put it on tape, and mounted two Bose speakers on a cart. The cart goes back and forth, passing Southampton several times a night and tooting into people's windows."

"You mean the cart doesn't have any passengers on it?" I asked.

"Not paying passengers," she said. "Of course it has conductors. Under terms of our union contract, there must be a minimum of 17 conductors playing pinochle and discussing their pension benefits at all times. But in terms of paying customers, no, there's just the whistle."

I learned that in its advanced state of decrepitude, the Long Island Rail Road's only remaining asset is its whistle, and they plan to franchise it to other companies so that they can keep people awake at night, too. "The Jitney has expressed interest," said the woman, "and so have several local cab companies."

She said the whistle-blowing program has been so successful that the LIRR is planning to extend it throughout the rest of the day and do away with the riding public altogether. "Think of the savings," she said.

The Jitney

Far more popular than the Long Island Rail Road is the Hampton Jitney. That's that ubiquitous green bus you see all over the East End and on the streets of Manhattan. People prefer it because it makes so many more runs and is more reliable. But it has its drawbacks.

For one thing, it lacks legroom. I am 6-foot-3, and I find riding on the Jitney about as comfortable as riding in an orange crate.

For another, it lacks light. If you want to read something, particularly at night, you have to bring a candle.

But the most distressing thing is the cell phones. Let's talk about that.

Not long ago, I was traveling into New York on the Jitney and the man behind me started to talk on his cell phone.

"Hello, Max?" he said. "Ray. Just thought I'd check in to see what's happening. . ."

Now, this is against the rules as posted by the Hampton Jitney (more on that later), but at the time, I was trying to read a book—*The Brothers Karamazov,* by Fyodor Dostoyevsky. I love *The Brothers Karamazov.* I read it in college, and have read it several times since. It's not that I'm particularly learned or anything; I just like books about God and patricide.

In *The Brothers K*, I particularly like the scene where Ivan corners Alyosha in a restaurant and delivers 20 pages on how Christ would have fared during the Spanish Inquisition. This is a famous chapter called *The Grand Inquisitor* and seems particularly relevant in the age of Antonin Scalia.

But it is very difficult to read if you can't concentrate, and that means you can't have neighbors yakking in your ear.

"No, I didn't think so," Ray was telling his friend. "Nothing ever happens on Monday. . ."

In *The Grand Inquisitor*, Christ returns to earth in the Sixteenth Century and is immediately arrested by the Cardinal of Seville. The cardinal recognizes that Christ's behavior is at odds with the Church, so he says Christ will have to be crucified again.

You can appreciate that this is a rather difficult concept to grasp. It is particularly difficult when Ray is telling Max, "Nothing new to report here, either. We've just passed Flushing and are heading for the tunnel."

In the chapter called *The Grand Inquisitor*, Christ learns that Christianity has changed so much He can no longer meet its requirements. The chapter is filled with passages like this:

> Hast Thou the right to reveal to us one of the mysteries of that world from which Thou hast come? No, Thou hast not. Thou mayest not add to what hast been said of old, and mayest not take from men the freedom which Thou didst exalt when Thou wast on earth. Whatever Thou re-

> vealest anew will encroach on men's freedom of faith; for it will be manifest as a miracle, and the freedom of their faith was dearer to Thee than anything in those days fifteen hundred years ago.

As you might appreciate, that is extremely difficult to absorb when Ray is telling Max that now we're at Fiftieth Street and heading toward Bloomingdale's.

Because Ray was nice enough to share his conversation with me, I got to re-read the above passage ten or eleven times. It mingled with news of Ray's bursitis, his winning hand at poker, and a quick rehash of the previous night's Islanders game.

I have since talked with the people at the Hampton Jitney, and they tell me that there is supposed to be a three-minute time limit on cell phone conversations.

"You mean if there are 50 people on the bus," I said, "you could have two and a half hours of nonstop talk?"

"Well, yes," they admitted. "But then we don't always enforce the rules."

They certainly didn't on my trip. Ray talked from the Midtown Tunnel all the way uptown and was still talking when I got off at Eighty-ninth Street. To make things worse, there were constant interruptions as everyone else's cell phone went *beep-beep* in response to incoming calls. I've never known so many indispensable people.

I have read that in England the railroads are coating their car windows with a microscopic metal in order to block cell phone transmissions. Isn't that a great idea? I think the Jitney should coat all of its windows with a microscopic metal, then coat Ray too. As he lies there, eyes glazed, I'll read *The Grand Inquisitor* to him.

Speonk: A Gothic Tale

I mentioned a place called Speonk. You probably thought I was trying to blow my nose, but actually Speonk is a hamlet on the far western edge of the South Fork, and I am one of the few people who has ever gone there and come out alive.

The occasion was an order from our then Town Supervisor (who preferred to be known as the Chief Poobah and Lord High Potentate of the Realm) to go to people west of the canal and sound them out on the subject of bike lanes. You see, I had gone to the Town Board and said I thought we should create more bike lanes so that cyclists could come out here on weekends and not get killed. The Chief Poobah said he thought that was a good idea, only I'd have to include the western part of the town in my planning.

Now, here I should explain that there is a canal that runs through Southampton and the people who live east of it know absolutely nothing about the people who live west of it. I mean, the East Siders assume that the West Siders are nice people and all, but they really don't want anything to do with them. And the feeling is mutual.

One of the communities that lie west of the canal is Speonk, and of all the strange and forbidding places, none is more strange and forbidding than that. Think of it as a kind of Transylvania stuck on the rump of Palm Springs.

So one dark and stormy night I struck out to carry the message to Speonk. As I stood on Hill Street, the wind whipping the trees and a thick fog drifting over the moors, I thought the coach would never come.

Then, out of the gloom, a light appeared, and I could hear the heavy clops of hooves. Thank God, I thought—and in another minute the coach hove into view.

"Aye?" said the coachman, leaning down and eyeing me with one suspicious eye.

"I'm in need to go to Speonk," I said. "Our Town Supervisor, Chief Poobah and Lord High Potentate of the Realm, has asked me to go talk to the people there about bike lanes. I'll pay you 20 pieces of silver for your service."

"Speonk!" replied the coachman, barking a huge wad of phlegm from his thin and bony throat. "No good can come from going to Speonk! I'll take ye only as far as Remsenburg! After that, ye're on yer own!"

Crossing the canal, we found ourselves in a progressively strange and barren place. There was nary a croissant shop or latte bar in sight. Mothers pulled their urchins from the road, and I could see from their frightened faces that these were wretched souls, incessantly subjected to the pressures of fast food chains and strip mall development.

Through Quogue and Westhampton we raced, the landscape growing more forbidding with each mile. Finally, outside of Remsenburg, we stopped.

"This is as far as I go!" cried the coachman. "T'ain't fit for Christian souls to be in Speonk!"

I paid him for his services and, continuing on foot, made my way across the windswept moor. Soon I espied an inn—a sad and lonely place, not the sort of place Starr Boggs would want to own.

I knocked on the door, and an innkeeper appeared.

"I come from out east," I said. "The Town Supervisor, Chief Poobah and Lord High Potentate of the Realm, has sent me to speak to you of bike lanes."

"The Supervisor!" came a roar, and when I looked inside I saw that the room was full of Speonkians.

Lowly, ill-clad people they were, many with warts and wens, all eating clams and talking in duck-like tongues. Not the type to land a reservation at The Laundry, I wagered.

"What does the Town Supervisor know of us?" they asked. "He never comes to these parts."

"He wants to know if you want bike lanes," I said. "In a place called North Haven, out beyond the Shinnecock Canal, there are beautiful bike lanes as far as the eye can see! They stretch all the way from Sag Harbor to the Shelter Island Ferry! He wants to know if you'd like lanes like that in Speonk."

"We are but simple folk," they said, "clam-diggers who respect the laws of God and Nature. What do we know of such high-flown things?"

"But bike lanes are beautiful!" I said. "You can ride them all day and not get hit by a BMW!"

"What's a BMW?" they asked.

I told them that there were people east of the canal who would be appalled at the terrible conditions in which they lived. "Why, when Charlotte Ford hears that you are living in a village without a single London Jeweler. . .when Martha Stewart hears that your women often have to go for days without a Citarella truffle. . ."

"Oh, your snobbiship!" they cried. "Those people don't care about us. We are but lepers who will never see a Wolffer Estates gala in our lives!"

"But you can have bike lanes!" I said. "You'll be able to ride safely on your humble conveyances to places like the Big Duck!*

---

*A 20-foot-tall by 30-foot-long hollow concrete duck on Route 24 which, according to TV personality Rosie O'Donnell, was "where everyone in high school went to have their first sexual experience." This may explain a lot about Rosie.

It will be for you what President Bush's nation-building was for Iraq!"

That stumped them.

"What must we do in return?" they asked.

"Nothing but swear eternal fealty to the Town Supervisor and allow a little roadside striping."

And so it came to pass. The peasants made their primitive X-es on the parchment, and now even Speonk may get bike lanes. The courtiers in Town Hall, taking time out from tossing their free-range chicken bones to the hunting dogs that grovel at their feet, will give those simple folk the same amenities we have on the eastern side of town. And that will mean their children can grow up strong and free and their babies won't have scurvy and they can pedal their humble three-speed Schwinns to the Coach Outlet of their choice.

East End Weather

One of the challenges of living on the East End is trying to figure out what the weather will be. That's because we have what's called a "microclimate", meaning that our weather is so personal that each homeowner needs his own password to access it. I can leave my house in Water Mill and by the time I get to the store I'll have gone through six people's personal weather fronts. They'll range from subtropical to hurricanes with hail.

If you're a cable subscriber, your Weather Channel's information comes from Islip—which is a very long hour and many storm fronts away. If you're a satellite dish user, like me, your

Weather Channel comes from God-knows-where. You may turn on your television and get twenty minutes about rain in Des Moines.

None of these reports has any relevance to Water Mill, which in turn has no relevance to Sagaponack or Amagansett. Since we've been known to have an occasional nor'easter around here, I went to Radio Shack and got a box called "The Weather Cube." This thing has an on-off switch and an antenna that pulls in round-the-clock weather forecasts.

My Weather Cube gets only three stations, two of which are static. But by moving a little dial on the back, I can hear a voice coming from somewhere out in the ether, giving me news about blue fish and tidal disasters.

When I use my Weather Cube, I'm reminded of those old World War II movies in which French resistance fighters exchanged transmissions in bombed out basements near Marseilles. I can picture Nazi patrol trucks with rotating antennae closing in as they try to triangulate on me.

The signal from my Weather Cube is so weak, I have to hold it against a screen door to increase its reception. Even then, I can only faintly hear a disembodied voice saying that a giant tsunami is moving toward Quogue.

I have a friend who used to do P.R. for the Weather Channel, and he tells me they're very nice people. They probably are. But I find a lot of their practices annoying. For example, they're always promising to be "right back" and never are. "Coming up: More on those tornadoes bearing down on Flanders. We'll be right back." Then you get six hearing-aid commercials and more computerized music than any human being can tolerate.

Worse is their international weather. Presumably, this is for travelers who want to know what to expect for an upcoming trip abroad. But here's what they'll hear: "Flurries in England. Warm in India. Rain in Nepal. We'll be right back."

For the life of me, I can't figure out what kind of traveler wants information like that. Nor are their graphics any help. You'll see a giant snowflake over Scotland, orange squiggles near Calcutta, and slanting lines on Outer Mongolia. You won't see anything about any place else, because the weather girl is standing in front of it.

I don't know why, if we can put a man on the moon (which we used to be able to do but probably can't now), we can't deliver more accurate weather forecasts. I'll spend half a day trying to find out whether it's safe to go out without my galoshes. But ask me anything about Des Moines. I know that town like the back of my hand.

The Water Problem

One thing the East End does not have to worry about is water, at least its quantity.* We're surrounded on all sides by the stuff and our annual precipitation usually creates many more runoff and drainage problems than drought problems.

*Well, not so fast. That used to be true, but beginning in the summer of 2010, dire water alerts were issued by the Suffolk County Water Authority. They were particularly upset with homeowners in Southampton's Estate Section who routinely use thousands of gallons of water to irrigate their lawns at night. All of which might suggest that you should either let your lawn die or restrict your house hunting to houses with private wells. Of course the well may get struck by lightning or go down in a hurricane, but at least you won't have to listen to water alerts.

But that doesn't mean we don't have issues. Most of the people on the East End have private wells, and these are fed from a large aquifer that runs along a moraine in the center of the South Fork. As you might expect, somebody is always trying to destroy this moraine and somebody else is always trying to stop them. That's the kind of morality play we have out here.

But there are other threats to our water. Our bays undergo periodic invasions of something called the Red Tide, which kills all the marine life; our ponds get polluted with agricultural and lawn chemicals; and our wells get threatened by Temec, which was a chemical once used to kill potato-destroying nematodes. All this leads to a certain amount of legitimate concern, which in turn can lead to out-of-control hysteria.

Some years ago a Long Island woman named Jane Gitlin read in *Newsday* that the rate of breast cancer in Nassau County was 13.5 percent above the state average while the rate in Suffolk County was 12 percent above it. Having the kind of keen scientific mind Long Island housewives have, she concluded that it must be something in the water.

She and a group of like-minded women decided to emulate the methods of AIDS activists and start threatening all the local politicians. They would go to town meetings and campaign rallies and demand to know what the pols were going to do about this obvious threat.

In one rather startling example of pseudo-science, Ms. Gitlin produced a map showing that breast cancer had claimed the lives of more women living at the end of dead-end streets than in the middle of them. The reason? The drinking water doesn't flow as fast at the end of the street. I tell you, with minds like Ms. Gitlin's, we can all sleep easier at night.

There are several weird things about this. First, despite the patent absurdity of their claims, these women actually managed to scare the politicians into supporting an expensive government study which, when it failed to confirm the ladies' hypotheses, drove them into even greater fits of rage. Second, in one recent year the government spent $550 million on breast cancer—more than on all other cancers combined—even though heart disease kills ten times the number of women and lung cancer kills one and one-half times as many. Moreover, of the women who do get breast cancer, 70 percent survive, while only 17 percent of lung cancer patients do. But I have yet to see a pink-ribbon campaign or 6-K run on behalf of lung cancer victims.

Still, there are several private and governmental groups tasked with the protection of our water, one of which is the Southampton Board of Trustees, created by a quaint statute called the Dongan Patent.

This is a piece of parchment that was drawn up by King James II of England back in 1686, through his General Governor, Thomas Dongan. It gave Southampton Freeholders access and rights to common underwater land and wetlands, with a board of trustees to act as enforcers. This board still exists. It has five members, typically all men and typically Republican. But how well they protect our water is a matter of debate, since another of our environmental watchdogs, Group for the East End, often criticizes them for being more lax than King James might have wished.

We also have Bay Constables, who go around in cute boats and act as our aquatic policemen, and something called the Peconic Bay Keeper who, like Paul Revere, raises the alarm when there's a threat to the crabs.

Last but not least, there is the Nature Conservancy, which is also active on the East End, and the Peconic Land Trust, whose concern is not so much water as land but whose heart is in the right place even if its style is more on the order of "Can't we all get along together?"*

Against this, we have the usual suspects of real estate developers, farmers (yes, farmers; farmers have a history of not caring as much about fish as about how much their land will be worth when they go to sell and move to Florida), and a bunch of other interests who tend to think that this is just a bunch of clam-cuddling foolishness foisted off on us by Al Gore. They know that what's really important is money.

Anyway, now you know everything you need to know about our water in order to impress that chick you just met at Conscience Point. She will be truly wowed by your grasp of these local issues. Only if I were you, I wouldn't get into that breast cancer thing. I doubt if it will serve the interests you have in mind.

The Casino Question

One of the most hotly debated issues on the East End is the Shinnecock tribe's desire to build a casino. They think it would be a wonderful idea, but almost no one else does. I have been giving it some serious thought and think I have a solution.

---

*Actually, what the Peconic Land Trust does is try to negotiate deals between property owners, developers and environmentalists. They try to point out the various tax incentives a seller or developer would have in not going hog wild with construction. Later in this book, I describe a 21-house development that went in behind my house. John Halsey, president of the Peconic Land Trust, tried desperately to convince the developer that he could make just as much money, and sell the properties faster, if he built just five houses. But the man wouldn't listen, so we ended up with 21 houses, some of which are still on the market years later.

As you may have read, in addition to chasing their casino dreams, the Shinnecocks have been pursuing a claim for 3,600 acres of real estate west of North Sea Road in Southampton. They claim that they were hoodwinked back in 1859 when local officials persuaded the state legislature to turn over their land to the whites so that the whites could build a railroad, and there's evidence that the Shinnecocks are right.

Still, that was a pretty good deal for us whites. The Shinnecocks got 750 acres of community-held land that denied them the possibility of ever getting mortgages, and we got 3,600 acres upon which to build a railroad whose toilets don't work.

Scholars say the Shinnecocks have a good chance of prevailing. If they can prove that the deal was indeed rigged, they might get real estate that includes three golf courses, all of Southampton College and a Burger King. Then they can proceed with their scheme to build a casino.

This sends shivers through the white community, which thinks that a casino in the Hamptons would be about as welcome as a strip mining operation in Yellowstone Park. But let's consider it in a more positive light.

Should the Shinnecocks win, they might be willing to sacrifice their casino dreams for something even more lucrative and with better public relations value.

What if, in place of a casino, they were allowed to build tollbooths across the Sunrise Highway on their newly acquired land, taking half the proceeds for themselves and leaving half as a charitable donation?

Stretching across the highway on new reservation land that would extend all the way from the canal to the 7-Eleven, it would have a broad toll plaza and high-speed E-Z Pass lanes that would let cars pass without slowing down. Each car would be charged

$1 for entering the Hamptons and another dollar for leaving. (Or maybe it would make more sense to charge them $2 for entering and let them leave for nothing. Sounds good to me.)

If you're a Hamptons resident, you'd be exempt. You'd simply present your car registration at the Shinnecocks' trading post, much as you do now at Town Hall for a beach permit, and they'd give you a little gizmo that fits on your windshield and allows you to zip through without charge. If you aren't a Hamptons resident, too bad.

Of each toll, half would go to the Shinnecocks and half would go to land preservation. In this way, the Shinnecocks would become richer than their old rivals, the Pequots, and everyone would enjoy a Hamptons that had some open space and a modicum of untainted water.

Moreover, the Shinnecocks would be able to line their coffers without exploiting human greed. There would be no temptation for fathers to spend their children's lunch money at the crap tables, and little old ladies would not be tempted to squander their Medicare co-payments on slot machines. The Shinnecocks would be seen as the saviors of the South Fork.

I've racked my brain trying to think of the negatives to this, but frankly I can't find any. Donald Trump would be happy (Atlantic City would remain unchallenged as the Empire of Sleaze), our mom-and-pop stores could keep selling Lotto tickets without competition, and traffic would be such that everyone could get to work on time.

In short, everyone would be delighted, and the Shinnecocks would be viewed as modern-day Santa Clauses. Rich Santa Clauses.

The way I picture it, the sign above the toll booths would read:

ATTENTION, MOTORISTS!

This Hamptons experience is brought to you
courtesy of the Shinnecock Nation.
Enjoy it, be out by Monday, and take your trash with you.

Now, admit it. Isn't that a great idea? Sometimes I stand in awe of myself.

The Incompleat* Angler

No guide to the East End would be complete without a description of the local fishing scene. That's why this guide is not complete. I know nothing about the local fishing scene.

But that doesn't mean I won't talk about it. As you may have noticed by now, the less I know about something, the more I have to say, and that includes things like fishing.

My idea of fishing is to go to a store like the Clamman, point to a fish and say, "I'll take that one." Then I go home and say to my wife, "You should see the ones that got away."

But a couple of years ago I signed up as a volunteer with the Big Brothers Big Sisters of Long Island program, and the Little

*No, that is not a misspelling. If you were an English major, as I was, you would know that *The Compleat Angler* was a famous book by Isaac Walton. But as you are about to discover, like you, I never read it.

Brother I adopted was keen on fishing. That meant I'd have to try to learn something.

I went to a bait-and-tackle shop in Hampton Bays and they set me up with a couple of cheap bamboo poles and a packet of frozen bait. They told me to go down by the inlet and drop a line in and I'd catch more snappers than I'd know what do with.

I followed their instructions, and spent the rest of the day waiting for something to happen.

See, here's the thing about fishing: As a sport, it is right up there with NASCAR racing as the most boring way to waste an afternoon. Yet, wherever you go on the East End, you will find dozens, if not hundreds, of people doing it. They'll be doing it on the beaches, on the docks, off the decks of boats. And when you say, "How's it going?" they'll say, "Oh, they never bite here at this time of year," which will tempt you to ask, "Then why are you standing there like a ninny with a pole in your hand?" But to do that would be like asking a Lotto player why he's wasting money on something he'll never win. It's just not polite conversation.

Still, I suppose fishing is better than staying home and watching your toenails grow, so we shouldn't be too hard on the poor devils.

The other thing about fishing is that people love to talk about it. When I walked into that bait-and-tackle shop and asked what I needed to get started, I thought it would be like walking into a country club's pro shop and asking the difference between a wood and an iron. I mean, I knew *nothing* about the sport.

But to my surprise, that didn't faze the owners at all—in fact, they seemed to take pleasure in the fact that I was so ignorant. I was an empty vessel into which they could pour their hard-earned knowledge. (A friend of mine who's an avid fly fisherman told me that the only thing a fisherman loves more than standing around with a rod in his hand is *talking* about standing around with a rod in his hand. So unlike when you, say, sit down with strangers in a game of five-card stud, you should not be afraid to show how stupid you are.)

And that's all I have to say on this subject, except to add that for years my wife, who knows as little about fishing as I do, has tried to get the local fish stores to put up signs advising customers when the various fish are in season. She figures that would help housewives with their meal planning. She's even volunteered to print up the information herself and provide it to the stores to give to their customers. What more could they ask for?

Every single store she went to said, "Hey, that's a good idea!" then said they were too busy to make out a list. After a couple of years of that, she gave up.

So now you know as much about fishing as I do. Aren't you glad you bought this book?

Weekend Shopping

Moving out of the fish stores… East End shopping can be a hassle, particularly on summer weekends. Some years ago my wife and I came up with a wonderful idea. We decided to start a shopping service for weekenders. We would call it Shophopper.

This was in the days before FreshDirect and Peapod, and what we proposed was to do weekenders' shopping for them and have all the food delivered to their homes by Friday night. Isn't that a great idea?

Of course there were details to be worked out. We would ask the customers to fax us their orders and give us the keys to their houses. After all, we couldn't leave ice-cream on the front porch, could we?

They would register their credit cards with us, and we'd do all their grocery shopping. We'd leave it in their fridges (we got ourselves bonded for protection), then charge the bill to their credit cards. The customer would receive a copy of the receipts, and we would tack on a fee of 20 percent.

Sounds good, right?

Well, there were several things we hadn't figured on. One of them was that weekenders are nuts. I don't know why, but there seems to be a requirement that if you're a Hamptons renter you have to have a screw loose somewhere.

One man called about our service and got irate because we wouldn't pick up his dry-cleaning. A couple in Sagaponack insisted that we use the Wainscott Fish Store instead of the Bridgehampton Fish Store, despite the fact that the former was miles out of our way. When we said no, they said, "Sorry, we only eat Wainscott fish."

We got a call at 11:30 one night from a woman in Montauk wanting to know if we could pick up a loaf of bread and run it out to her by midnight. Guess what we said.

We had a client who said she found our service so good she decided to stay out for the month of August instead of traveling back and forth. "I never knew how much fun it could be out here until you relieved me of the shopping," she said. But since now she was staying out for the month, she had no further use for us. We said thanks a lot.

The main thing wrong with the idea was that, while people don't want to do the shopping themselves, they're not willing to compromise on the slightest thing for the sake of service.

One of our clients had a cat. This cat was the Felix Unger of cats. According to the client, the cat would only eat Fancy Feast gourmet cat food and only specific flavors on specific days. It would eat turkey on Monday, cod on Tuesday, beef on Wednesday, and so on.

Now, if you're familiar with Fancy Feast cat food, you know that it comes in these little teensy tins in about a zillion flavors. Although each can costs only 50 cents, the Fancy Feast section of the supermarket takes up 25 feet of shelf space.

So every Thursday morning found me standing in the pet food aisle going through hundreds of tiny cans trying to find the seven specific flavors that stupid cat would eat for the week. And don't think I could cheat. When I came back with chicken once instead of turkey, the woman had a fit. The cat, she claimed, would never forgive her.

Right Flavor, Wrong Day

It finally occurred to us that this was not a profitable operation. It was taking me half an hour to find the seven flavors that cat would eat at a net cost of $3.50. My profit was 70 cents, not including gas and car depreciation.

I still believe a shopping service is a good idea, and maybe someone will figure out how to do it properly, but it won't be me. Meanwhile, I'm working on a scheme to turn Long Island Railroad station houses into bicycle rental shops so that week-enders can get off the train, bike into town, then return to the train without getting into anyone's hair. Sounds good, eh? I think so, too.

More Shopping News

Since we don't have the big chain stores and discount malls other areas have, bargain-hunting women on the East End have to be resourceful.

My wife is a bargain-hunter. She wouldn't think of buying anything without checking out TJMaxx. I swear, if we were in the market for a new car, she'd check out TJMaxx.

But in her world, there's shopping and there's Shopping. Lower-case shopping is what you do at King Kullen or Rite-Aid. Upper-case Shopping is what you do up-island with your friends.

It has long been noted that men and women don't shop the same way. Men go into a store, buy something, then leave. That's because the only store men are willing to spend more than five minutes in is a hardware store. I'll come home from Herrick Hardware or Water Mill True Value and say, "Look at this great wing nut I found! Isn't it a beauty?" My wife will say, "But you already have a basement full of wing nuts." I'll say, "Yeah, but this one's *stainless*!"

If you can't find it in a hardware store, you don't need it. If my wife says I need a new sport coat, I'll say, "I'll stop by True Value and see what they've got."

But what my wife does with her friends is Shop, capital S. The magnitude of these excursions falls somewhere between Edmund Hillary's assault on Mount Everest and the Allied invasion of Normandy.

First, the logistics. A____ (the women don't want their names used for obvious reasons) will call to say that she, L____ and E____ want to go to Syms.* Would my wife like to join them? That's like asking a barfly if she'd like a nightcap.

Then follow days of planning and preparation. Whose car? What time? Which additional stores? What route?

The women realize they only have sedans. These are deemed inadequate to the task. They'll need at least a station wagon, perhaps a semi.

I drive an Outback. It has a nice roomy rear end with one of those handy pull-out gizmos that conceals your cargo. They'd rather have an Econoline, but since beggars can't be choosers, they'll take my Outback.

Watches are synchronized. L____ calls to say that she'll pick up A____ at 9 sharp, then swing by E____'s house at 9:04. They'll arrive at our house at no later than 9:17:36, and my wife should have the motor running.

Objectives: Syms, Marshall's, Costco, God-knows-what. I ask if they're going to Tanger. My wife sneers. "There's no time for Tanger when you're going to Syms," she says.

When these women hit a store, they're like army ants. Nothing is left intact. In the dressing rooms, they're brutal with each other. "You can't wear that!" they'll scream. "You look like a toothpick in an inner-tube!"

---

*A discount clothier popular among women. Their motto is "An Educated Consumer Is Our Best Customer," but apparently there weren't enough educated consumers on Long Island to keep the store open that my wife and her friends liked to go to. That has sent them into a permanent state of mourning.

My wife says she gets more insight from these trips than she'd ever get from a psychiatrist.

Come the big day, she's up at dawn. A serious Shopper takes her own lunch. A serious Shopper lives on rations in the field—yogurt, salad, Evian, hardtack.

"Do you have plenty of water?" I ask. "I don't want to hear you've died of thirst outside of Liz Claiborne."

"We aren't going to Liz Claiborne," she sighs with a look that says, "How often do I have to explain this to you?"

One of their firm rules is, No Men. That's because we men don't get it. If a man shops with his wife, he'll say, "What are you looking for? A blouse? Here's a blouse. Now, let's go."

Women *hate* that. They view shopping the way they view reading a P.D. James mystery. It's not how it turns out that's important; it's the process of getting there.

The other firm rule is, Never Pay Full Price. That's something I can never grasp. At the end of the year, my wife will have spent $47,462.83 on necessities. I'll have spent $52.34. But I'll have paid full price. When Ferdinand Marcos questioned Imelda about all those shoes, you can bet she said, "What are you crabbing about? They were discount!"

"When will you be home?" I ask.

"Don't wait up," she says.

I make sure she has a flash light, emergency flares and a first-aid kit.

"You'll find chili in the freezer and salami in the fridge," she says. "Adios, muchacho!"—and with that, she's off.

Usually, she gets back by nightfall.

"How did it go?" I'll ask.

"I didn't really find much," she'll say, struggling to lug her huge Syms and Marshall's Megastore bags over the door sill. "But look what I got *you*!"

She pulls out a Home Depot bag.

"What is it?" I ask.

"A wing nut!" she says.

"Oh, boy!" I say.

"It was on sale," she says.

Women Are From. . .You Know

I have noted that men and women don't shop the same way. Actually, they don't do anything the same way, including telling a story. When my wife tells a story, she starts in the middle, strikes out fore and aft, and ends up somewhere south of the punch line. When I tell a story, it is concise, witty and by all accounts brilliant.

Let's say we're at a dinner party and, in order to liven up the conversation, I say, "By the way, who knows why the chicken crossed the road?"

This is a hilarious anecdote and one that I tell very well.

At that, my wife will pipe up and say, "Oh, yes, do tell why the chicken crossed the road to get to the other side! It's hilarious!" (It's at this point I wish she had gotten lost at Syms.)

These are the things that try husbands' souls. I'll say, "Well, now that you've ruined it, why don't you tell the story and I'll just sit here and listen?"

"Oh, but you've been telling it for 25 years," she'll say. "I wouldn't dream of spoiling your fun."

Here one reaches a crossroads that is crucial to any marital relationship. Should the husband smile gamely and proceed with his now-pointless story, or should he pick up a carving knife and plunge it into his wife's head?

I'll say, "Okay, why did the chicken cross the road?," and at that the woman sitting across from me will say, "What kind of chicken?"

Now, I have been victimized by this sort of nonsense for years. Women can't keep on message. If you're trying to tell a story, they'll invariably interrupt with some irrelevant question.

"Who cares what kind of chicken?" I'll say. "This isn't a story about chicken identity. It's a story about a generic chicken crossing a generic road."

"Well, if it's anything like the chicken I bought at Waldbaum's," she'll say, "you'd better check the sell date because it could be spoiled."

At that, another woman will jump in. "Oh, don't you just hate that?" she'll say. "I had the same thing at King Kullen. It wasn't even past its sale date, and when I opened it, it was yucky!"

"We're not talking about supermarket chickens!" I scream. "We're talking about a live chicken crossing a road for reason or reasons unknown!"

"Maybe it was to escape becoming a capon," my wife will say.

"Why do you say that?" I'll say.

"Well, maybe it knew what the farmer had in mind and was trying to escape castration."

"We're not talking about castration!" I cry, my own voice rising to that of a soprano. "We're talking about a road crossing!"

"I've been thinking of having our cat castrated," the woman across from me will say, "but I'm not sure I have the heart."

"I know what you mean," another will say, "although they say it's for their own good."

"Hey!" I cry, pounding the table. "We're trying to tell a story here!"

"Oh, don't be like that," my wife will say. "You know, Ren

was an only child. Whenever you interrupt his chicken joke, he gets furious."

"You're the one who asked me to tell it!" I croak. "If you'll let me proceed, we'll all have fun!"

"Well, you're taking too long," my wife will say.

"I'm taking too long because you keep interrupting!" I cry. "If you'll stop interrupting, it won't take so long!"

Why men and women should have these problems, I don't know, but I think it may be for the same reason that, when we go to bed at night, I turn the thermostat down and my wife turns it back up.

"Why are you doing that?" I say.

"Because it's freezing," she says.

"Fifty-eight is not freezing," I say. "Thirty-two is freezing."

"Feel my feet," she'll say.

"The fact that your feet have been dead for 20 years does not mean it's freezing," I say. "You can put covers on your feet. I can't peel the skin off my body."

"Then warm my feet with your back," she'll say.

"Awk!" I cry, and leap out of bed.

They say women are from Venus and men are from Mars. That may be. But if so, it's because the people on Venus have cold feet and don't know how to tell a story. No man would want to live on a planet like that.

It's Not the Merchandise—It's the Yarn

Back to the problem of shopping…

Because of the East End's remoteness from the civilized world (we often get mailers from stores in Connecticut urging us to shop there, oblivious to the fact that there's a large body of water we'd have to cross) we sometimes have to resort to catalogs. And here's where the difference between men and women becomes even more profound.

Pick up a woman's catalog and you're likely to read something like, *You can never have too many shoes. Here are more.*

That makes sense to women, because they are genetically descended from centipedes. There is not a closet in our house that is not full of my wife's shoes. But to anyone of the male persuasion, that marketing is insultingly uninspired. Not only does a man who owns two pairs of shoes not see any reason why he should own more (he's got one of brown and one of black), but he is totally uninterested in any shoe that does not have a *story*.

Men love merchandise with *stories*. They don't care what tomfool thing it is—they'll spend their money on nerf-ball guns and mink-gripped monkey wrenches—but they want to know whether it's got a good, macho pedigree and (this is most important) what Chuck Yeager had to do with it.

I have before me several catalogs from companies like Russell's For Men, Leichtung Tools and Griot's Garage. They all read pretty much the same. Here's a typical piece of copy:

> Every man needs a pair of toenail clippers, but not those cheap things you get at Target. We first came across our Retro-Turbo Toenail Severing Tool while snowbound with Chuck Yeager's mechanic in a lean-to on Mount Kilimanjaro. No ordinary clippers, these were made of the finest Solingen steel and meant to withstand the rigors of torrid desert heat and supersonic flight. The mechanic informed us that they were one of only three pairs left in the world.
>
> We despaired of ever finding them again, but last year,

> in a small sampan off the coast of Burma, we came across a craftsman who was still making these remarkable tools. We asked him if he would make some for us, and he agreed.
>
> Built to our exacting specifications, these Toenail Severing Tools will not only separate the toughest nail from the strongest foot but, thanks to their titanium-filled mallet handles, they will help you smash through the windshield of an armored personnel carrier submerged in ten feet of water. There is also a 20,000 candlepower halogen light in the handle to signal rescue aircraft. Yes, they cost a little more—we're letting ours go for just $349.99—but once you've tried them, you'll want a second pair.

The tradition of this kind of copy goes back at least as far as LL Bean, which used to talk about their "bird-shooting pant". LL Bean is the only company I know that ever offered buyers a singular pant. I think you had to specify which leg.

Bean's catalog would say how they had field-tested their bird-shooting pant through five Maine winters and found it superior to any other pant on the market.

My latest catalog from Griot's Garage is selling quartz-crystal tiles to line your garage floor—and boy, what a story!

These babies are 2 ft. x 2 ft. tiles "made of quartz ground into chips and mixed with 7 percent polymer resins and color pigment," says the catalog. Griot tested them by rolling over them "with a 48,000-ton tractor-trailer rig." They also pounded them with hammers, dropped heavy wrenches on them and submerged them in the same acid that ate away Vincent Price's face in *House of Wax*.

No, I'm only kidding about that last, but they do make it clear that anyone who isn't willing to spend a year's salary to line his garage floor is a hopeless wimp, and probably in favor of gay marriage.

This got me to thinking of how a Victoria's Secret catalog would read if it were written by a men's catalog copywriter:

> We first came across this little lace thong on a Eurasian nymphet playing volleyball in Ipanema. When we asked where she got it, she said it had been specially made by an S&M dominatrix who learned her trade in a Cuban detention center.
>
> We thought it so charming that we brought it back and added details of our own. These include an environmentally friendly hemp strap that lassoes both nipples and holds them erect while a state-of-the-art Ben Hogan graphite filament encircles the neck and hooks behind each ear.
>
> Field-tested by Mrs. Chuck Yeager in the Detroit Lions' locker room, it makes the perfect lounging outfit after a hard day's work.

Now that baby would move!

A Shopping Tip for Men

As I said, men and women do not have the same approach to shopping, and since there aren't that many men's stores on the East End, the man is often forced to buy his clothing out of a catalog. Generally, this works okay as long as he gets his wife's approval, but if he doesn't, it can lead to serious discord.

Recently, I decided I needed a new sport coat. The black-and-brown hound's-tooth that had looked so good on me in the seventies was getting a bit long in the tooth (ha-ha). I still have fond memories of when I bought it and thought it made me look like

Mike Connors in *Mannix*. Remember *Mannix*? Weak plots, strong jackets.

But I find fewer and fewer people refer to *Mannix* now, so I decided to upgrade. Not wanting to travel a hundred miles to fight my way through Bloomingdale's, I went to the catalogs.

As I've mentioned, I have no shortage of catalogs. I get catalogs from soldier-of-fortune outfitters trying to sell me camouflage pajamas, golf companies trying to sell me socks with Greg Norman's picture on them, landscaping companies wanting to sell me a log-splitter capable of taking on a forest of California redwoods. One of the catalogs I get comes from a clothier named Joseph A. Bank. I knew Joseph A. Bank had a big store on Madison Avenue near Brooks Brothers, so how could I go wrong?

Well, you're about to find out.

When I called the 800 number, the operator didn't raise a flag. She didn't say, "Sir, before we proceed, I need to ask you, have you asked your wife? You really should, you know." No, she just took my order, asked for my credit card number and said, "Thank you. Have a nice day."

A few days later, the coat arrived. We were going out that night, and I decided to wear it. I put on my best pants and shirt, then slipped on the coat.

"Well, what do you think?" I said, spinning around several times in the front hall so that my wife could appreciate it from all angles.

"How much did you pay for *that*?" she said.

I think that was my first hint that not all was well.

"Actually," I said, "it was on sale. They said they had an overstock."

"I can see why," she said.

I decided to wear it anyway. I thought that if she got used to it, she'd change her mind.

Wrong.

"I've seen better-looking straitjackets in a nuthouse," she said. "I've seen Mafia victims who look better in their cement overcoats. I've seen refrigerators that look better in their boxes. Who designed that thing, SpongeBob SquarePants?"

I said, "Maybe it needs a little tailoring."

She said, "What it needs is incinerating. It makes you look like a sofa treated with Scotch Guard."

After listening to this for several weeks, I said, "Well, if it's that bad, I'll give it to the thrift shop and buy another one."

"Don't you dare!" she said. "You're George Bush, and that is your Iraq. I want you to wear it as a reminder of your limitations. I think you should wear it to the Maidstone Arms and have all the men with taste fall off their barstools laughing. I think you should wear it to Nick and Toni's and have Billy Joel come up and say, 'I've seen better clothes on a clamdigger in Peconic Bay.' I want you to wear it to Paul's Pizza and have them say, 'I'm sorry, sir, but we *do* have standards.'"

I don't remember Mannix catching this kind of grief. Mannix had a very nice secretary named Peggy. Remember her? She never told him he looked like SpongeBob SquarePants or a sofa treated with Scotch Guard. Mannix had a habit of getting sapped on the head every week and waking up in a car that was hurdling down a mountain without any braking fluid. Still, he always looked great.

My wife says she's going to bury me in this jacket. She says she wants everyone to walk past my open casket and see what a blunder I made. She says she may even reproduce it on my gravestone. In fact, she says it *looks* like a gravestone.

I guess the lesson is, Always ask your wife. I know I will from now on. Although I did see a nice-looking double knit in J. Crew the other day—and they say the Nehru collar is coming back.

Speaking of Caskets...

I was interested to note in a recent Rockler's woodworking catalog that for just $14.99 I could get a "Wood Casket Plan" that would enable me to build my own casket at home.

As a guy who likes to plan ahead, I couldn't help thinking, how better to spend an inclement East End weekend? After all, if it turned out well, I could build one for my wife, my dog and my neighbors. It might be a nice little sideline.

I went on Rockler's website and learned that for $247, plus shipping, I could get everything I needed except the lumber. The hardware would include lid hinges, lid supports, mattress spring and mounting hardware, metallic corners, handle brackets, handle ends and something called a "memorial tube". I guess I could stuff my newspaper columns in that.

As my wife pointed out, the Little Missus could do the upholstering.

When you think of what a funeral parlor would charge, doesn't that sound like a good deal?

Also on the website was a review by someone who had actually built one of these things. His name was Curtis Vixie, and he said he lives in Susanville, California.

In his review, Mr. Vixie explained that he was not building the casket for himself but for a "friend who will be using it in a few months." Whether the friend was aware of this need was not mentioned.

Mr. Vixie said he made the coffin out of a red cedar tree from the friend's back yard, a process which he admitted "added a fair amount of time" to the project. I can appreciate that. Particularly if the friend didn't want his tree cut down.

Mr. Vixie seemed pleased with the results and included photographs of the finished product sitting in his backyard. One can imagine how thrilled his neighbors were.

I'll admit, my interest in this was piqued by having recently gone to a woodworking show in Springfield, Massachusetts. There, I saw all sorts of fascinating do-it-yourself projects.

I had always wanted to go to one of those shows, and when a flier arrived announcing that there would be one in January, I told my wife that I was going. I didn't ask her permission, I just asserted my manly prerogative.

These shows are amazing. They had all sorts of classes on everything from router techniques to tool sharpening. I spent three days learning how to apply finish, turn bowls on a lathe and even make my own Japanese wood plane, should the urge arise.

But they did not teach me how to make a casket, which I think was too bad because I would have certainly sprung for it.

Not to worry, though. For $14.95 Rockler will sell me a book called "Do-It-Yourself Coffins", written by Dale Power with Jeffrey B. Synder. According to the catalog, the book uses color photographs to "illustrate every step in building coffins" for yourself or your pet.

Unfortunately, the reviews for this book were less than glowing. On the Web, Jack Middendorf of Cincinnati called them "poorly made boxes that looked like they were put together and finished by children." Jason Fritz of West Mifflin, Pennsylvania, said, "The author should be embarrassed." But on the positive side, there's obviously a market for this sort of thing, so one hopes some future author will step forward to meet the demand.

In the meantime, I guess I'll have to choose some other project. Here's a book on how to make padlocks out of wood. Those should be useful. And here's one on how to build a statuette of a cow with a jigsaw cutout of a calf fetus dropping out through the cow's bottom. That might look like nice on our mantle.

But back to those caskets. One wonders what you're supposed to do with them between the time you've finished building them and the time you're ready to climb in. Do you sleep in them, like the Bela Lugosi character in *Ed Wood*? Do you use them as a coffee table? Perhaps you can stand them upright in your front hall and use them as a place to hang your guests' coats.

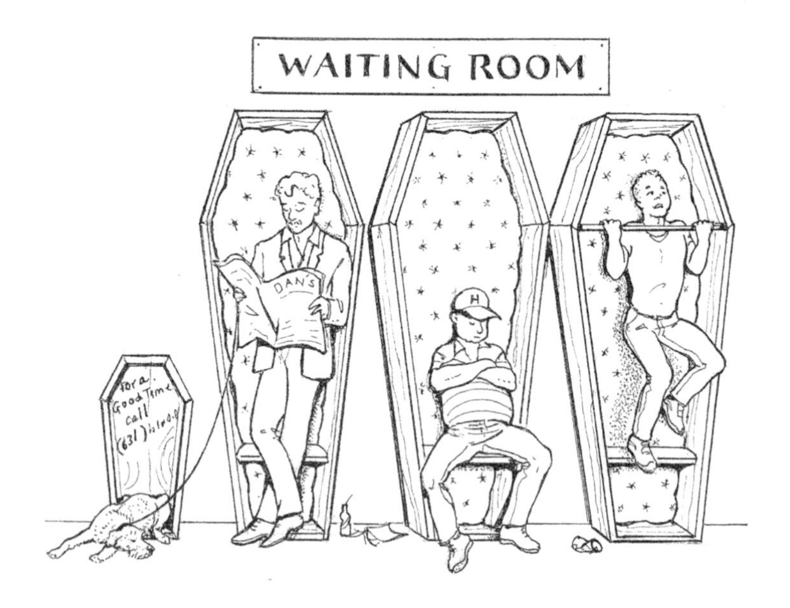

The Wise Do-It-Yourselfer Plans Ahead

Well, we may never know, because I'm going to give up the casket idea and make a wooden xylophone instead. Caskets take up too much space, and I was planning to be cremated anyway.

Your East End Personal Christmas Shopper

Every year, as a service to readers, I go through all the Christmas catalogs that come in and select those items I think will be of lasting interest. (Remember: I cut my teeth at *Reader's Digest,* whose motto was "An article a day of lasting interest.") Here is a list of some of the things I've found.

From the Vermont Country Store you can order a product called Wrinkies and Frownies, which are described as "small adhesive patches" that "diminish wrinkles on your forehead or corners of the eyes and mouth" and make you "look like Arlene Dahl."

Now, for those too young to remember, Arlene Dahl was an actress in the Forties and Fifties who may or may not still be alive. She was almost, but not quite, as popular as Faye Emerson. Whether she's alive or not, Wrinkies and Frownies will make you look like her. Some might say that the Vermont Country Store is a little behind the times, but when you learn that the New Hampshire Country Store is touting a product to make you look like Lillian Gish, you see how really up-to-date Vermont is.

Here's something for all you red-blooded he-men from *Griot's Garage Handbook*. It's the "Six-Speed Blockage Clearing Toilet Plunger", and it's made to look like a real racing car's gearshift.

Just think of the fun you'll have crying *"Vroom! Vroom!"* as you clear the loo with this Mario-Andretti-style gearshift-cum-suction-cup. It's only $29.95, and would be a bargain at twice the price.

To liven up that next dinner party, *The Greatest Gift Catalog* is offering a large dinner table that's actually a bass drum. Yes, covered with genuine calfskin, it comes with four drum beaters so you can sit around and pound out "dramatic bass tones" while your guests are trying to eat.

Imagine the surprised look on their faces when they sit down to bouillabaisse and you start banging out the Ohio State Fight Song on the drum-table. Better still, you can get a pair of "Rhythm Stix" from The Sharper Image* that will "let you get in touch with your inner Ringo." These sticks have built-in speakers that "blast out techno-tom-tom beats, crashing cymbals and spectacular snare sounds." The Drum Table costs only $589.95, and the Rhythm Styx (complete with brilliant blue flashing LED lights) are a steal at $19.95.

As usual, Hammacher Schlemmer has some of the best bargains. "The Peaceful Progression Wake Up Clock" for $49.95 is a favorite. It "uses a gradual increase in ambient light, stimulating aromas and peaceful sounds from nature to awaken sleepers." According to the catalog, 30 minutes before wake-up the light begins to glow softly, then the lamp releases aromatherapy scents, and finally the clock begins emitting sounds like "a crashing thunder storm." It makes a great companion piece to the "Precise Time Ceiling Projector Clock", which projects the time onto your ceiling so that you can lie awake and see how much sleep you're losing while waiting for the thunderstorm. Both can be had for $109.90, plus shipping.

---

*See, and you wondered why they went out of business!

Speaking of lying in bed, Hammacher is offering "Back-Saving Horizontal Reading Glasses" at $39.95. These allow you to lie on your back and watch TV without raising your head. In beautiful tortoiseshell plastic, they have two prism lenses that protrude from your forehead like periscopes. These allow you to watch TV while remaining oblivious to the Ceiling Projector Clock that's clicking away your life overhead.

Just in time for winter, Skymall is offering a "Blizzard Sport Portable Snowmaker" that will allow you to have all the fun of living in, say, Buffalo. Yes, even if it's another disappointing global-warmed winter, with your Blizzard Sport Portable Snowmaker you won't miss a single day of shoveling. It costs only $2,495—which, admittedly, is about the same as a trip to Aspen, but you'll have snow and your neighbor won't.

Mother's Little Helper

Saving the best for last, both Hammacher and Hard-to-Find Tools are offering a "Self-Navigating Sweeper-Vac" that will clean your house while you sleep or watch TV. Imagine the fun you and your dog will have as this small-but-powerful vacuum whizzes around your house, knocking over chairs and sucking up everything in sight. It's only $200.00, and for an additional $29.95 you'll get an infrared "Virtual Wall" which will keep the Sweeper-Vac from flying out your front door, crossing the street and devouring your neighbor's cat.

Is this a great country or what?

Those Obnoxious Ads for Dads

All this shopping talk reminds me of how much I hate Father's Day. (I'm sorry if I've gotten a little off the subject here. We'll return to life on the East End in a moment. It's just my attention deficit disorder kicking in.) It's not the day so much as the ads. Publications like *The New York Times* and the trendier weeklies feature male models who, if they were really fathers, would say a great deal about the decline of Western Civilization.

Who would want to go to one of these guys for help with your homework? They all look like they're barely out of high school themselves.

The kids they're pictured with seem to be about six years old. Do the math. The ads are urging first-graders to buy Movado watches for 19-year-old slackers who are too lazy to shave.

It makes you wonder what's in the advertisers' minds. The fathers appear to represent everything narcissistic and irresponsible. Most of them haven't combed their hair in days. They're looking into the camera with that typical Madison Avenue sneer, wearing outfits that might consist of a tuxedo jacket, torn jeans and beach sandals. Is this the kind of guy you want to call Dad?

To me, a dad should look like Gregory Peck in *To Kill a Mockingbird*. You never saw Gregory Peck in torn jeans with his hair uncombed. He certainly didn't wear his shirt outside his pants or appear without socks at a board meeting.

The thing about fathers is that they're supposed to look *dependable*. They're supposed to look like the kind of guy you can go to and say, "Dad, could I borrow the car tonight?" and he'd say sure, but only after a stern moral lecture.

That's what Robert Young did in *Father Knows Best*. He said, "Yes, Bud, you can take the car, but do you realize the responsibility you have to drive safely and not turn the radio up?" That's the kind of dad you need.

The guys in these Father's Day ads look like Ben Affleck after a hard day's night. If you asked them if you can take the car, they'd stare at you trying to remember who you are, then say, "Sure, take the Jag, but try to be back next month."

Stores like Bloomingdale's and Macy's seem to think this image sells. They aren't going to be happy until every six-year-old scrapes up enough dough to buy Pop a new Armani suit. What Pop will do with that suit is anybody's guess, since he seems to have an aversion to looking well-groomed. He'll probably rip the knees out and wear it with beach sandals.

Not that Mother's Day is much better. Chances are, your mother looks like Barbara Bush, but come Mother's Day, all the moms look like Britney Spears.

These models aren't mothers, even if they have children. They're just manikins with no connection to the real world.

Do you think a mother who looks like Britney Spears would ever do anything so unglamorous as have a baby? Even if she got pregnant, she'd hire a Mexican to have it for her.

These ads are symptomatic of everything that's wrong with our society. While the fathers look like gigolos and the mothers like go-go dancers, the kids look like pint-size Hotchkiss graduates who have no resemblance to either parent. The boys wear

Paul Stewart blazers and British public-school ties and the girls wear granny dresses that make them look home-schooled. Meanwhile, Dad can't afford a razor.

These WASPy kids and their dissolute elders are always sitting around what looks like a Bar Harbor clambake, smirking. They're not interacting, just smirking. There's no feeling of affection between them, just privilege.

I think the admen who created these ads never had children. They certainly never had parents. When they came out of the womb they must have looked at the people who conceived them and said, "Forget it. This'll never sell."

Think of all the great TV mothers and fathers that kids used to look up to: Ozzie and Harriet, John and Olivia Walton, Homer and Marge Simpson.

Well, okay, maybe not Homer and Marge, but the point is, can you imagine any of those people sitting around a Bar Harbor clambake getting a Rolex from a brat in a blazer?

This just goes to prove that fashion ad writers are the most sophomoric, scrofulous, hypocritical people on earth, with the possible exception of movie reviewers, pop music critics and sports writers, and we'll talk about those next.

Dodson's Inferno

There is a special place called Dodson's Inferno, which is a hellish venue reserved for people who have annoyed me.

If you were to see it, you'd find it crammed with politicians, bible thumpers, Chamber of Commerce members, telemarketers, reality show producers and the creators of *Beavis and Butt-*

head. They are all fated to meet their unpleasant and very just reward.

The lowest realms of this Inferno are populated by four types of writers: fashion writers, movie reviewers, pop music critics and sports writers. Let's maul them one at a time.

The trouble with fashion writers is that they all have amnesia. Having convinced you last month that you should narrow your lapels, raise your hemline, trash your ties and ditch your furs, this month they tell you to do the opposite. They all have Alzheimer's.

"At last," they'll sigh with that bloviation for which they are so notorious, "Karl Lagerfeld has seen through the staidness of last year's trends and introduced the kind of free-and-easy look we've all been waiting for."

Baloney. Nobody's been waiting for anything. Whatever Karl Lagerfeld designed last year was no more or less wearable than what he designed this year, which is to say not very. The only thing most people are waiting for is a new Land's End catalog.

Movie reviewers are no better. I've long pitied those poor dolts who dropped out of grad school because they thought Fellini would be easier to understand than Chaucer. They sold their souls for what they thought would be a glamorous career of flashing cameras and red-carpet premiers, only to be plunged into a miasma of *Die Hard* sequels and *Big Momma's House*.

Actually, there is no sense sending those poor devils to hell since they're already there. They spend all their waking hours in darkened screening rooms watching junk no one over the age of 14 would want to see.

The only way they can justify their existence is to make it sound as if the movies are important. They're very good at that. They'll take the silliest Jim Carrey flick and turn it into an existential treatise. You'll have to read it ten times to understand what it says, and even then the only thing you'll know for sure is that the reviewer is very, very hip.

You see, hipness is what counts to a movie reviewer, and in my Inferno they're all condemned to watching *The Blair Witch Project* for eternity.

Then there are the sports writers. You've heard the adage "He who can't, teaches"? Well, sports writers prove that "He who can't hit, writes."

What I find particularly annoying about sports writers is their tendency to moralize. Face it, athletes aren't saints. If you want clean living, go to the Dalai Lama. But these writers will uniformly rise in high dudgeon if John Rocker says something silly about New York or Jason Giambi admits to having chewed arrowroot before an archery tournament.

And remember, these are the same writers who condemned Muhammad Ali for refusing to serve in Vietnam and who think a player is being just a little spirited if he tries to strangle his coach. They'll get offended by the slightest political incorrectness, but if you try to tell them that a three game suspension for aggravated assault is too lenient they'll call you a prig.

Then there are the pop music critics. These are people who can't understand classical music, so they try to elevate the Sex Pistols to the level of Mozart.

They'll write something like: "Just when Nutz2U seems about to capitulate to the clichés of Weltanschauung, their coda transforms into a paradigm suggestive of their authenticity in the urban Zeitgeist."

Bloody hell! They're rockers, for God's sake! They wouldn't know a paradigm if it fell on them. What happened to rock as the people's music? Would Chuck Berry worry about his Weltanschauung?

When the history of our era is written, it will be said that never has so much pretension been heaped on an entertainment vehicle of so little consequence. After all, for all their urban Zeitgeist, Nutz2U will sound to the next generation just like Rudy Vallee sounds to this one.

So these are the lowest of the low and will be so treated in my Inferno. You will find them down there living out their miserable eternities in unspeakable agony.

Of course there may be others down there with them, such as opinionated newspaper columnists, but we're out of time, so let's return to life on the East End.

The Great Pine Barrens Fire

Weekenders might be interested to know that there's an area on Long Island called the Pine Barrens. Perhaps you've seen it while driving out on the LIE. It's that long, boring stretch in which you can't find a single Starbucks.

A few years ago, it burned down. Not only did it burn down, it almost took the village of Westhampton Beach with it.

All that was well covered in the media, but what was not well covered was how the fire started. It was started by Martians.

A little-noted story in *The New York Times* reported that a man named John Ford from Bellport had been arrested for conspiring to kill some Suffolk County officials he thought had suppressed information about the Pine Barrens Fire.

According to Mr. Ford, these officials had purposely and willfully refused to tell the public that the fire had been started by Martians who had crash-landed their UFOs and were now holed up in Brookhaven National Laboratory. He tried to kill the officials by putting radium in their cars and lacing their toothpaste with radioactive metal. (As Dave Barry would say, I am not making this up.)

At the time, people in places like Kansas and Nebraska said, "Where do Long Islanders come up with this stuff?" Californians, ever jealous of anyone who tries to wrest the Wacko Fruitcake Cup away from them, said, "That's what you get from Joey Buttafuoco's crowd. They're mad because we've still got Kato Kaelin."

Well, those critics are snickering out the other sides of their mouths now. I can confirm that not only did Martians start that fire, but according to NASA there really are extraterrestrials on this planet, and some of them may have arrived in meteorites made to look like potatoes. (Again, I am not making this up. This story was also reported in *The New York Times*.)

According to *The Times,* there was a NASA scientist named Dr. Roberta Score who found "a potato-sized meteorite" in Antarctica, which was subsequently labeled ALH84001. She said she had found it while she and her friends were "cruising around having fun," and that this meteorite might have housed Martians.

Astute journalist that I am, I called the Johnson Space Center and asked what evidence they had that Martians arriving in potatoes might have put the torch to our Pine Barrens. To me, the connection seemed obvious: potatoes + Martians = Pine Barrens Fire. But I could tell from the silence on the other end that NASA was not prepared for this line of questioning.

"What are you talking about?" they said. "What are the Pine Barrens?"

I knew, of course, that this was the kind of ploy public officials use to stall for time when they've been found out. They like to answer questions with questions in the hopes that the journalist will start talking about *his* problems and forget why he called.

"Don't be coy," I said. "We have a man rotting in jail here who was trying to save our planet. His only crime was to try to get Suffolk County officials to come clean and tell us about the Martians. Now, I can't put it any clearer. We have a lot of potato-sized objects lying around here, and we have a lot of women cruising around having fun. You don't have to be a rocket scientist, if you get my drift, to see the link."

It's at times like these that you feel rewarded being a journalist. You can ask the really tough ones and not feel guilty about it.

"Well," they said, "we never said we found any Martians, and we certainly didn't say they arrived in potatoes."

"Oh, cut the you-know-what!" I scoffed. "Are you saying it's pure coincidence that a fire breaks out in the middle of potato country and we've got Antarctic spuds with the skeletons of Martians in them?"

By now my face had assumed that leery, raised-eyebrow look so familiar to viewers of *60 Minutes*. It's the look that says, Who do you think you're talking to, Mister Rogers?

"They weren't skeletons," said the NASA spokesperson, "and we never said it was a real potato. What we said was that we found something that are possibly Martian fossils imbedded in something the size of a potato."

At this point, I dropped my Mike Wallace look and assumed my Raymond Burr-Perry Mason look, the one Perry always wore when he was about to nail the guilty party. "And what would you say," I asked, "if I told you I have evidence of a physical link between these creatures from Mars and what's been going on in the Brookhaven Laboratory?"

In *Perry Mason*, this always worked beautifully. It inevitably resulted in a tearful confession in which the culprit broke down and spilled everything. Afterward, Perry's secretary, Della Street, would say, "Perry, what evidence were you referring to?" and Perry would say, "I didn't say I had any evidence, Della. I asked what he'd say if I *said* I had evidence."

In this case it didn't fly. "You're nuts," the spokesperson said and hung up on me.

There is obviously more to this than meets the eye. I'd say the case needs further investigation, and I may ask my colleague Karl Grossman to look into it. But if what I suspect is true, those Unidentified Flying Spuds will make the space ships in *Independence Day* look like small potatoes, and the creatures inside them like Joey Buttafuoco.

Cluster Housing

Some years ago, in an attempt to fool weekenders into thinking there was still some open space on the South Fork, our town introduced a concept called cluster housing. This was a policy that allowed the developer to despoil whatever land he wanted, as long as it was up against the houses of people who already live here. That way, there'd at least be a strip of bulrushes separating the new McMansions from people driving by in cars on their way to buying up more land.

My own house fell victim to this unhappy policy and one day I woke up to find a new development going up in my backyard.

Needless to say, I was not too thrilled. I had not moved out here to be surrounded by other people's Gunnite pools and tennis courts, so I protested. But it did no good. Southampton's Planning Board said that if I gave it a chance I'd see what a wonderful improvement it would be.

You might be interested to know that in the parlance of East End town halls that's what developments are called—"improvements." Unimproved land consists of woods, crops and pheasants. Improved land consists of asphalt, houses and swimming pools. The implication is that when the Indians had the land, it was a mess. It took the white man to straighten things out.

I was slow to catch on. When surveyors appeared in my backyard and started driving in stakes with orange ribbons, I asked if these were some of the "improvements" I could expect.

"Oh, these are just the beginning," said the surveyor. "Wait till the blacktop and Belgian blocks arrive."

Actually, I found their Day-Glo markers rather pretty. The unimproved land was kind of somber—beige, green, brown. The improved land was dotted with festive ribbons.

A few weeks later, I was startled by the sound of bulldozers in my bedroom.

"What are you doing?" I cried to the burly man whose machine was snapping off tree trunks outside our window and ramming them into a chipper.

"Making improvements!" he shouted. "Wait till you see! You're gonna love it!"

"You may be surprised," I told him, "but only last month we picked blackberries in those woods."

"Ha ha!" he laughed. "You won't have to worry about getting those seeds stuck in your teeth now! Ain't nuthin' gonna grow here for 50 years!"

The next day, I noticed that he had cut down half my front yard.

"That's a misconception," said the town engineer. "The road in front of your house has a 65-foot right-of-way. You thought it was your yard, but it wasn't—it was ours. We need your yard to put in the leeching pools."

"What are leeching pools?" I asked.

"Storm drains to handle all the flooding you're going to get once we've improved the land." And sure enough, over the next few weeks I watched as 95 leeching pools got buried in the fields around my house. These 12-foot-deep cylinders had concrete domes and black manhole covers and were a great improvement over the previous row crops.

"Will you leave my mailbox?" I asked.

"Sure," said the engineer. "We'll need that to measure the depth of the floods."

The following week began with what I call the "Battle of the Bulge." That was when a Panzer division of steam shovels and earth-moving equipment moved through our living room.

"Sorry to disturb you!" cried the man atop the giant Kamatsu. "We're putting in more leeching pools today!"

"This is going to be a great improvement," I told my wife as we stared at the Kamatsu shredding our fence posts to mulch at six in the morning. "Remember those trees that kept dropping leaves all over our yard? Now there'll be nothing out there but manhole covers. Think of the labor it will save."

The real estate agent handling the subdivision told me this was the best thing that could have happened to me. "We're going to increase your property value threefold," he said.

"You mean, people will spend more to look at the driveways of new houses than at a farm field?" I asked.

"Sure," he said. "BMWs trump potatoes every time."

So I apologize for all the nasty things I said about our town's pro-development mentality. They were right in insisting that the developer put 21 houses behind me. In fact, I'm going to invite all the people in Town Hall to come and join me for a wine and cheese party so that they can look out at all the wonderful new McMansions back there. The storm drains are particularly lovely this time of year.

The Great Hamptons Clearances

As popular as the Hamptons are, if you live here you'll soon hear that everyone's leaving. Where are they going? Oh, North Carolina, Florida, Maine, Arizona, you name it. It's like the Great Scottish Highland Clearances. As Yogi Berra might have put it, Nobody lives here any more because it's too crowded.

When I go out to get our morning newspaper I'm often met by an early-rising walker who lives about a mile away, and every morning tells me he's leaving. "Look at all these houses," he says, stopping to talk to me by my driveway. "I'm selling out. This place is ruined."

He's been telling me this for four years. I have no reason to doubt his sincerity, but what's taking him so long?

When I wrote an article suggesting that it might be a good idea, as proposed by a group called Five Towns Rural Transit, to replace the Long Island Rail Road with a shuttle service that runs every half hour, I got an e-mail from a woman who said, "If that happens, I'm leaving. Trains every half-hour would be a nightmare."

My suggestion that she stick around and try to make sure Five

Towns Rural Transit did right by her fell on deaf ears. Working things out wasn't her bag. Threatening to leave was.*

You may wonder why, with so many people leaving, there's so much building going on. Well, I can explain that.

The builders are tired of having nothing to do. They have a lot of leftover nails in their nail guns, so they go around looking for lots to build on. It's cheaper than taking the nails back to Riverhead.

Don't be surprised if you go to the supermarket one day and come back and find a new dormer on your house. The builders are driving around, and when they see a house that looks unoccupied, they put a dormer on it. It doesn't make any difference whether you wanted the dormer or not; they've got their nails, and the traffic is bad.

A Member of The Committeee Against Everything

---

*This woman no doubt belonged to a very powerful group out here called The Committee Against Everything. The Committee Against Everything meets on a rotating basis in various community centers and voices its strong opposition to whatever is being proposed. If someone wants to put up a new stop sign, they're against it. If someone wants to take down a stop sign, they're against that, too. I have compared them with my dog MacDuff, who, when he sees a trash bag sitting where it hasn't been before, barks at it. After several days he accepts it, but then, if it disappears, he's upset about that, too. Dealing with this committee is one of the few constants of life on the East End.

You may wonder, Well, if this place is so unpopular, why is the traffic so bad?

I think I can explain that, too.

The traffic is a conspiracy concocted by the realtors at Corcoran and Brown Harris Stevens to make us think people want to live here, when they really don't. The people driving around are out-of-work builders who are being paid five dollars an hour to make the Hamptons look popular. They come from places like Comack and Shirley and drive around with their cell phones and nail guns, clogging up our roads.

I haven't tested this, but I think if you walked into a Corcoran or Prudential office and asked how much they really wanted for that piece of waterfront property, they'd say you could have it for ten bucks. "Eight million was just the asking price," they'd say.

I'll tell you this: I'd leave here myself if I had any idea where to go. They say Nevada is nice, but the sand is so far from the surf.

Last Affordable Waterfront Home

A School Bond Voter Speaks Out

If you live here year round, you know that one of the major bones of contention every election year is school bonds. A large portion of our taxes goes to support our schools, and a lot of people don't like that.

Recently, I talked with a typical East End voter about this problem, and here's what he said:

> Yeah, well, the school board's trying to stuff another one of them bond issues down our throats. When'll they learn? We can't afford to waste all that money on schools.
>
> I was saying to Traci just last night, I go, "Traci, they're tryin' to ram another one of them bond things down our throats. Pass me the nachos, will ya, hon? What do they think, we're made of money? Listen to this. According to the newspaper, they claim their classrooms are fallin' apart and the kids need a decent food service. *Food service!* Hello! Can anyone tell me WHY?"
>
> Of course, Traci hates it when I interrupt her in the middle of *American Idol*. Particularly since we got our new TV. High-Def, Surround Sound, plasma, the works. You should see it. Two thousand bucks.
>
> I go, "TiVo it, baby. We got to get out there and vote that thing down. These people are givin' away the store!"
>
> Traci goes, "I understand most of the people who vote against them things are, like, retirees, you know?"
>
> I go, "No way. I ain't no retiree, and I'm votin' against it."
>
> She goes, "They say the retirees are votin' against it cause they got no kids so they don't care if the schools fall apart."
>
> I go, "Traci, I'm 42, I got a kid, and no one cares less about the schools than me."
>
> Traci goes, "What about Jason?"
>
> I go, "Who's Jason?"
>
> She goes, "Our kid."
>
> Oh, yeah. I remember Jason. He's the one the other kid threw a ball-four at last year in Little League and when the umpire called it a strike I went out and punched out the umpire's lights. Nothin' I wouldn't do for that boy.
>
> I go, "What about him? Toss me a Bud."

She goes, "Well, he says they got like plaster falling on their heads and the school could use some new paint and stuff."

I go, "Traci, haven't we given Jason everything he needs? Xbox, iPod, GameBoy, the works? What does he need a classroom for? A little plaster never hurt nobody."

She goes, "Maybe we should vote for it just this once so the school stays open and gives him a place to like hang out, ya know?"

I go, "Traci, these teachers are robbin' us blind. They want pencils and books. *Books*, for God's sake! They only work a ten-month year. I wish I had it so easy."

She goes, "By the way, where is Jason? He hasn't come down for dinner."

That's another thing. Traci's a real good cook, you know? I mean, it's not just pizza and Big Macs every night. Sometimes she goes to Schmidt's and everything. But Jason, he don't always come down. Kids today, what can you do?

I go, "Isn't he in his room?"

She goes, "I dunno. I haven't seen him since Christmas."

I go, "Don't worry. I got him locked in on our GPS. He's up there, all right—he's watchin' TV."

Ever since we got him that new TV (56-inch screen—awesome, man) he spends a lot of time up there.

I go, "He's probably surfin' the Net, or maybe watchin' the World Federation Xtreme Hot Pants and Disembowelment Championship. It's on tonight, pay-per-view."

She goes, "Yeah, but his nachos is gettin' cold."

I go, "I'll ring him."

See, that's the thing. I spend a lot of time with my kid. Quality time. Teachers don't know.

I ring him on the cell. I go, "Yo, bro! What's up?"

He goes, "Who you?"

I go, "Your father, man. What's goin' on?"

He goes, "Way cool. They just ripped some dude's guts out, and now they're tearin' up the arena and callin' in the T-Rex Terminator. Whaddaya want?"

I go, "Your mother's opened some really awesome nachos down here. Why don't you come down and have a few?"

He goes, "I'm still workin' on the pizza she thawed."

I go, "Okay, bro, but that ain't a balanced diet. You need some nachos to go with that pizza."

Jason's a bit big for his age. Five-one, 165 pounds. That's kinda big for a nine-year-old, right?

I go, "Well, take care. See ya around."

See, that's what the school board don't understand. They want all that luxury stuff. We can't hardly afford the necessities.

Hey, Tax Assessor! You Dissed Me!

As noted, taxes are a major issue. This is particularly true among locals and year-rounders. Whenever there's a reassessment, they go bananas.

Recently, we had a major assessment and people got really upset. I did, too. They undervalued my house.

You see, there's a website called Zillow.com, where with a click of a mouse you can locate your house and get an accurate estimate of its worth. I did that and found that the assessors had undervalued me by 20 percent. How do you think that made me feel? That's right—awful.

According to an article in Forbes.com, my Water Mill Zip Code, 11976, is the sixth-most expensive Zip Code in the country.

I feel that if I'm living in a place this swanky, I should be recognized for it. When my tax bill comes in, I'm going to send in 20 percent more than is on the bill and let the town sort it out. If they don't like it, too bad.

Actually, I suspect Water Mill would have been the *most* expensive Zip Code were it not for my house. When people think they have to live next to a shack like mine with such low taxes, it depresses the market.

And what is the *most* expensive Zip Code in the country? Why, Sagaponack, of course.

With a median home sale price of $2.8 million, Sagaponack beats out Beverly Hills, Newport Beach and all those other fancy Zips. Water Mill's median sale price is only $2.4 million, probably because it's been dragged down by my under-assessment.

I can't tell you what this has done to my morale. I'm afraid that the mayor of Sagaponack will no longer speak to me. I'm not in his class. Heck, no one's in his class. His village is so expensive, if Mayor Bloomberg called and asked him to lunch at the Four Seasons, he'd have to say, "Sorry, Mike, but your real estate's too cheap."

I have it on good authority that Fox TV is working on a new series called *Sagaponack 11962*. It will have Luke Perry playing the mayor of Sagaponack and Tori Spelling as Marilee Foster.* Ira Rennert will be played by Gary Oldman in one of his maniacal modes.

I don't know the plot, but it will undoubtedly involve plenty of farm-stand infidelity and promiscuous rutabaga.

Of course here in Water Mill we're at least better off than Bridgehampton, which is ranked only 25th by Forbes. The me-

*One of the East End's best known farmers, and certainly its most literate. Anyone not familiar with her nature etudes in The *Southampton Press* should make it a point to become so.

dian home sale price in Bridgehampton is $1.6 million, which in Water Mill wouldn't buy an outhouse (although it would easily buy my house, should anyone be interested). I expect poor Dennis Suskind*, who lives in Bridgehampton, will have to apply for food stamps.

According to Forbes, Shelter Island Heights ranks 27th in the nation, and Amagansett and Wainscott are tied for 42nd. They have median sale prices of $1.5 and $1.4 million respectively.

That's not bad, but if you live in Sag Harbor, Quogue or Westhampton Beach, you're probably feeling you've made a terrible real estate choice and are living in a tear-down. Maybe you should move to some place with a future, like Detroit.

When I go to sell my house, I want Corcoran to be able to say: EXCLUSIVE! A GROSSLY UNDER-APPRAISED HOUSE IN ONE OF THE MOST EXPENSIVE ZIP CODES IN THE COUNTRY! When people see that, they'll say, "Wow, no wonder the asking price is running off the page!"

They used to do a lot of house moving out here. I wonder if I could pick up my house and move it to Sagaponack. Then Corcoran could run ads that say: BE PART OF FABULOUS 11962! RUB SHOULDERS WITH LUKE, TORI AND THE HOT RUTABAGA! BUT HURRY! DEALS LIKE THIS WON'T LAST!

---

*A former Goldman Sachs executive who has cut a curious figure on the East End. First, he volunteered to help counsel students at the perennially underperforming Bridgehampton School, then he served on the Southampton Town Board as a Democrat and environmentalist, then he threw his weight into development and became an anti-environmentalist. He is also a linchpin in the Hamptons Classic Horse Show and heaven knows what else. I like to think of him as a kind of East End Silvio Berlusconi, only without the sex scandals. At least not that we know of.

Advice for Oceanfront Homeowners

We had a mole problem this year. That's because of all the development behind our house. (Have I mentioned that?) The moles that used to live in the fields back there packed up and moved, and the place they moved to was our back yard.

This was not what we wanted. Moles are pesky little things that are very hard to get rid of, making labyrinths in your lawn and destroying your trees.

I tried everything, but nothing worked—sprays, traps, spikes, poisons. I considered buying one of those electronic thingamajigs that uses ultrasonic sound to drive the critters out, but I was afraid it would drive out my wife instead.

Finally, I bought a lawn roller. This was upon the advice of a professional pest control man, who told me, "Frankly, we aren't too good at getting rid of moles, but if you keep flattening their burrows with a roller, they'll get mad and go away." That seemed plausible.

I went to Home Depot and bought a lawn roller and spent the next two weeks going back and forth over the lawn. Every time a burrow appeared, I'd flatten it. After a few weeks—no burrows!

According to a young man who cuts grass in our neighborhood, the moles left our yard and went next door. "You should see it over there," he said, pointing to our neighbors' lawn. "It's a mess."

This raises the question of why moles are so much smarter than human beings. Look at the number of humans who build in flood plains or along the shore and have their houses destroyed again and again, only to return to the same place. Every time, they say, "Oh, this is terrible! We'd better move!"—but they never do.

As soon as the flood or the hurricane passes (or the earthquake or the wildfire), they build right back where they were before and wait for the next disaster. That's what a mole would call a "Duh!" response.

A mole would figure, "Hey, we've been burrowing in some place God doesn't want us. Let's get out of here and go where there's no lawn roller." His wife would say, "But it's the middle of the school year and junior will miss his friends." The mole would reply, "I don't care. I'm not going to stay here and get flattened everyday! What do you think I am, nuts?"

A Mole Takes a Hint

In my experience, yellow jackets are also smarter than humans. Every spring, our yard is a target for yellow jackets, or, as a local who is more familiar with these things calls them, sand wasps. They seem to be attracted by the nectar in our garden and the heat from our shingle siding. They build hives, and I get stung.

There's nothing meaner than a sand wasp who thinks you're endangering his queen, unless it's the homeowner who is told he can't build a revetment to protect his house against the next hurricane. When you destroy a sand wasp's nest, he gets mad and pulls a kamikaze on you. When you don't let the beachfront homeowner build his revetment, he sues.

But in the case of the sand wasp, he knows better than to rebuild in the same place, which makes him smarter than the beachfront homeowner.

The sand wasp says, "Okay, no more Mr. Nice Wasp!" and builds his next hive inside your barbecue grill. The following week, when you go out to grill a burger, you'll get stung again, but you will come to respect the wasp's ability to think, as it were, outside the box.

Of course the answer might be that the people who have built their homes on Dune Road or Gin Lane have spent a lot more money than the moles and sand wasps have, but that's debatable. In terms of real capital, I would wager that the mole and the sand wasp have spent just as much for their homes as the beach dweller has. While the beach dweller has shelled out cash, the mole and sand wasp have had to pay with the proverbial sweat of their claw or wing. Which makes them more prudent.

I think that if the oceanfront homeowners were told they had to rebuild their homes themselves—i.e., they'd have to get out mortar and a trowel and put in all the screws and nails themselves—you'd see a very quick migration.

The beach dweller would say, "Come on, Sibyl" (or Cheryl, or Courtney, or whoever the trophy wife happened to be that week), "Indianapolis has never looked better!"

This would level out the real estate market, decrease the

shoreline traffic, and return our beaches to the state nature intended. Then all would be right with the world, and the moles and the sand wasps, not to mention the rest of us, would be happier.

My Trophy Wife

Speaking of trophy wives...

If you're going to make any impression out here, you have to have a trophy wife. I do, and believe me, it has helped a lot.

Of course, if you have such a wife it makes other women angry. "Disgusting male pig!" women will often mutter as they pass me in the street. They'll often mutter this even when my wife isn't around, but I've gotten used to it. The fact is, her trophiness has been the key to my success, and I think every man should have a wife just like her.

Of course there is a downside. Those jealous women should take consolation in the fact that I haven't been able to talk to my wife in years. You see, I was born four years earlier than she, and that makes an enormous difference. I was born a little before World War Two and she was born during the war. That makes her—well, almost a Boomer.

Boomers don't know how to talk to us Silent Generation guys. I'll say, "Hey, this angel's food cake you made is really keen," and she'll say, "Keen? What's that?" I'll say, "You know—swell."

My wife doesn't speak prewar. I don't come by the lingo naturally myself, but in my day it was required if you were going to understand the Bowery Boys.

My wife doesn't know the Bowery Boys. She doesn't know who Kilroy was, either, or why it was so important that he be wherever he was. When she gets up in the morning and finds I've scrawled "Kilroy was here" all over the walls, she doesn't know why I did that.

"Ecausebay," I say, "I oughtthay it ouldway ebay unnyfay."

My wife doesn't know Pig Latin. In my day, you had to know Pig Latin. If you didn't know Pig Latin, you couldn't get into college. It was on the SATs. By the time she came along, the schools had dropped Pig Latin and were teaching things like Spanish. It was just part of the educational backsliding that was going on.

I say, "Atwhay oodgay is it to earnlay Anishspay in odaytay's ompetitivecay orldway?"

She just blinks. It's Pig Greek to her.

Regarding the word keen: When I explain what it means, she says, "Oh, you mean groovy! Why didn't you say so?"

Now, I know what groovy means. I'm not squaresville, you know. But when she throws a newfangled word like that at me, I'll say, "No, I mean nifty. I mean, George."

Living with my wife is like living with a teenager—or someone who was a teenager when I was 20. I was raised on Vaughan Monroe. My wife thinks Vaughan Monroe is ungroovy. "How can you listen to *Racing With the Moon*," she'll say, "when you could be listening to Petula Clark?"

Sometimes I have the feeling I'm living with a blank slate. I'll say, "Don't you remember how much fun it was sitting around after school watching Captain Video and his Video Rangers?" It means nothing to her. Her dawn of consciousness began with Howdy Doody. Forget all those great jokes by Milton Berle and Jerry Lester. She barely remembers George Gobel.

This generation gap influences our fashion. I like to wear my jeans the way they're meant to be worn, turned up about six inches at the cuff, like Gene Autry's. She wears hers like Peggy Lipton on *Mod Squad*. Peggy Lipton wore her jeans down around her hips and frayed at the ankles. I'll say, "You look like a beatnik in those." She'll say, "What's a beatnik?" That was before her time.

The other day I was sitting in my Barcalounger watching *Lawrence Welk Reloaded: The Director's Cut* when she came in and suggested we play backgammon. "You're not serious," I said. "At my age?"

Now, I used to play backgammon all night. Back in the seventies, when I was in my prime, I could play backgammon with three different women at the same time. But now, for this chick to taunt me with such a suggestion seems needlessly cruel.

I say, "The next thing you know, you'll want me to play the Boomer Edition of Trivial Pursuit."

I used to be pretty good at Trivial Pursuit, but when they came out with the Boomer Edition, I faded.

The Boomer Edition is for people who don't know anything. They think *The Brady Bunch* is a Homeric classic. When we play the Boomer Edition, my wife has the advantage because she knows the characters in *Happy Days*. I don't know the characters in Happy Days. I *was* a character in *Happy Days*.

One of these days I'll be on my deathbed reliving *Teresa Brewer's Greatest Hits* and my wife will waltz by on her walker, shouting, "Don't trust anyone over 80!" I'll turn down my hearing aid so as not to hear her.

She'll be wearing one of those tie-dyed hospital gowns with a picture of Che Guevara on the front, and I'll be wearing my zoot-suit pajamas with the pegged pants and a porkpie hat. I'll say, "Let's lindy," and she'll say, "Let's frug."

So, see, life with a trophy wife is not all it's cracked up to be. It may look good from the outside, but as Leo Gorcey used to say, it ain't all beer and skittles.

Trophy Wife, circa 2025

Thoughts While Picking Up Other People's Garbage

As you drive around the East End, you'll see a lot of Adopt-a-Road signs. These are signs posted on roads where local homeowners have volunteered to pick up the litter people throw out of their cars.

I'm a member of this program, which means I have spent a fair amount of time picking up other people's garbage. Every morning there's a new crop lining our road.

As I do this, I can't help wondering, Who's throwing out all this stuff and what on earth are they thinking? I believe this would be a worthwhile sociological study. Someone should track down these litterbugs and ask what was on their minds. It would make a good doctoral dissertation.

Every morning, I find another assortment of beer bottles, cigarette packs, Coke cans and Whopper wrappers outside of my house. That's in addition to all the old tires, bed springs, construction debris and deflated Open House balloons.

These things are in my yard, my drive, my trees. If I didn't know better, I'd think they were part of the natural flora. Maybe they come out with the sunrise, like day lilies.

I tried littering myself once, but it didn't work out. I was on a subway platform in New York and had a little piece of paper I didn't know what to do with.

I was carrying a briefcase and thought of putting it in there, but that seemed sort of awkward. I'd have to put down the briefcase, open it, drop in the paper, etc.

There was no trash can around, so I edged over toward a support beam and stealthily dropped the paper near my foot. The perfect crime!

Alas, no sooner had I done that than someone tapped me on the shoulder and said, "Pardon me, sir, but I think you dropped something."

Now, this was at the 42nd Street subway station. Trust me, there's nothing pristine about that station. But if a well-dressed guy drops a gum wrapper there, it's like one of those old E.F. Hutton ads: "When Reynolds Dodson litters, everyone listens."

Anyway, in front of my house a large proportion of what gets discarded once contained beer. There are more Bud and Colt 45 cans than there are fallen leaves. But not all the brands are so proletarian. I find Beck's bottles, Heineken bottles, Corona bottles, Guinness bottles. You got to hand it to the slobs—they've got taste.

Another thing I notice is that most of what's discarded is unhealthful. No one ever throws away a tofu wrapper or a yoghurt cup.

This leads me to wonder whether all the slobs are fat. Judging from the number of Big Mac boxes, Frito bags and Pringle's cans, the odds seem favorable.

But I've also noticed an ample supply of chicken bones. Chicken's not all that fattening, so who's throwing those drumsticks away?

This leads to thoughts of ethnicity. We've had a lot of new home construction in our area (have I mentioned that?), and many of the workers are Latino. Latinos seem to like chicken. I think they just haven't caught on to pastrami heroes yet.

There's hardly a bush or tree on my street that doesn't have a drumstick under it. I know, because my dog MacDuff has found them all. No true, red-blooded American would eat a drumstick for lunch. It would be too non-fattening.

While I'm thinking this, I'm thinking, What's the psychological profile of a litterer? Do they think that because a road has trees on it nobody lives there? Do they think that there's a litter fairy who comes out every night and picks up everything they've dropped?

One thing they don't seem to think is that a human being will have to clean up after them. Nor do they think that if everyone did what they're doing there wouldn't be any road left to drive on. There would just be Snapple bottles.

I don't know what to do about this, but I'm thinking of building a duck blind out by the road and sitting out there 24 hours a day with an assault weapon. If the Supreme Court strikes down local gun control laws, I could shoot every guy who comes by and tosses something out. Sure, a few innocent lives may be lost, but Antonin Scalia wouldn't mind. That's the price you pay to keep America beautiful.

Doghampton

I mentioned MacDuff, and that leads to thoughts about East End dogs. The first thing everyone does when they move to the Hamptons fulltime is get a dog. (That's right after they get a trophy wife. It's a tossup as to which will give them greater pleasure.) After all, this is the country (sort of), and dogs and country go together.

The three most common dogs on the East End are Labrador retrievers, golden retrievers and Jack Russell terriers. The first two go with water and pickup trucks, the third with blondes in riding jodhpurs.

When my wife and I moved here, we decided to get a dog, only we didn't choose any of those. We chose a Westie.

For those unfamiliar with that breed, Westies are terriers who want nothing to do with water or pickup trucks (although I don't think they have anything against blondes in riding jodhpurs). In fact, when a Westie sees a Labrador rush into the surf to retrieve a stick, he thinks that dog is in serious need of therapy. The Westie (whose full name is West Highland white terrier) knows that water is for ducks and retrieval makes no sense because once you've got the stick, it's yours.

What follows are some Westie-eye views of the East End. The first Westie you will meet is Tucker, who was very precocious. Would it surprise you to hear that Tucker was accepted into Princeton? Well, he was, and he would have gone there had he not decided to take some time off to gain emotional maturity. We told him that gaining emotional maturity was a worthy goal for a terrier.

So let's begin with Tucker's Credo, which he explained to me one day while yapping into a computer with bark-recognition capabilities.

❖ WHAT I BELIEVE ❖

By Tucker

- The best car ride is always the one coming up
- If you stand in the kitchen long enough, something will drop
- A human is never really happy unless he's scratching your belly
- Never let a squirrel into your yard. It will bury nuts and lower your property values
- There is no urine so good that the addition of yours on top will not make it better

Princeton Candidate Waiting for Something to Drop

- Never chew with your mouth closed
- A woman doesn't know if she likes runs in her stockings until she's tried them
- Feel goodwill toward all dogs except those larger than you
- Never let a cat into your yard. It will scare the birds away and lower your property values
- Never allow a human being to go out unleashed
- Remind your owner that he is the source of all happiness, whether he wants to be or not. Do this incessantly at all times of day
- Always face in the right direction before pooping
- Don't listen to those who say fireworks aren't bad. They're nuts
- A bone off the street is worth two in the bowl
- Never throw up without having a nice rug under you
- Don't let mailmen into your yard. They'll stuff your box with junk mail and lower your property values
- Anything worth having is worth burying
- No matter how bad your day, don't lose sleep over it
- When playing poker, never let them see your tail

- Don't listen to people who praise veterinarians. Veterinarians are horrible people, and you should run whenever you see one

There. And you thought Princeton had lowered its standards.

Dogs and Television

Tucker used to spend a lot of time watching television. Not unlike humans his age, he favored action programs and shows in which furry things leap through the air and run through the woods. He also liked cartoons. Whenever a cartoon came on, he would jump up and try to climb into the set.

It amazed me how smart Tucker was. He knew the animals were in that box, and he would go around behind it and try to get at them. For awhile we thought this was cute, until he learned how to operate our VCR.

This was something we never mastered. No matter how hard we tried, we could never get the darn VCR to record what we wanted. Once I managed to record three-quarters of a program before realizing I had forgotten to rewind the tape. I was in the middle of an Audie Murphy gunfight when all of a sudden Audie got lost in snow. What started out in Arizona suddenly turned into an Alpine blizzard. Another time, I might have recorded something had I remembered to put the tape in. That's an easy thing to forget when your entertainment center looks like a jumbo jetliner's flight deck.

Of course, until we moved out here full-time, our house had no TV at all. That sounds incredible, but it was a strangely halcyon place where one could spend whole weekends chatting, reading and listening to the local college radio station. But after moving here fulltime we realized that we had better start acting like normal people and get a television. That meant calling our friendly cable company.

The cable company on the East End is Cablevision, and they are a favorite target of scorn. The only company that's worse is Time-Warner Cable in Manhattan. Why these companies have been allowed to have such monopolies is beyond me, particularly when the judges were so hard on poor AT&T. AT&T wasn't bothering anybody, but the judges said, "Off with their heads!" I wish they would do the same to Time Warner and Cablevision.

Anyway, Cablevision was prompt to respond. They hooked us up in no time and things went well for a few months, until they changed their lineup and moved some channels to higher numbers. To our chagrin, we found that our VCR only went to Channel 48. We couldn't record anything higher.

"Ah!" said one of Cablevision's many helpful representatives. "That can be easily remedied by the addition of a converter box. We'll lease you one for $3.60 a month."

A few days later, a service man showed up and said, "Here's your converter box. Where do you want it?"

We said, "Oh, wherever you can find room between the TV, the VCR, the record turntable, the CD changer, the stereo tuner and the tape deck. We haven't bought a laser disc player yet."

With effort, he dug a little hole in among the wires and shoved the box into place. "Let's see if she works," he said.

He called his office and asked them to send a signal. I didn't know what that meant. I thought maybe it was some sort of death ray like they used to have in the Buck Rogers serials. In Buck Rogers, somebody was always sending a signal, and it did not augur well. But he assured me it was safe, and when he hung up, they sent the signal.

It didn't work.

"No problem," he said. "I'll come back later and with another box."

He was as good as his word, and that box didn't work either. "Sometimes these things are finicky," he said.

After the third visit, he installed a box that worked and said, "Now, let me show you how to use it.

"When you want to turn on your TV, don't turn on your TV, turn on your converter box. If you want to use your VCR, turn on your VCR, but not your TV.

"If you want to record something on Channel 50, put your TV on Channel 3, then push the 'Menu' button on your VCR. The menu will appear and ask what channel you want to record.

"Don't tell it you want to record Channel 50. Tell it you want to record Channel 3.

"After you've done that, tell your VCR what time the program will come on and go off. Only don't tell it the truth. If your show is coming on at 1, tell it it's coming on at 12:55. If it's going off at 3, tell it it's going off at 3:15. And always be sure to check your tape speed, because if it's too fast you'll run out of tape. Are you with me so far?"

"Of course," I said.

"That concludes step one. Now you have to program your converter box. To do that, press the 'Menu' button. On your screen you'll see a menu with three choices. Don't choose any of those. Choose the fourth choice, which you can't see, but which will give you the programming menu. Remember—always select the choice you can't see.

"Once you've done that," he continued, "you're ready to tell the converter box what channel you want to record. This time tell it the truth. Tell it you want to record Channel 50. It will acknowledge that, then ask you what time the program starts. That's when you lie again.

"Tell it an earlier time than when it really starts. Only don't tell it the time you told the VCR. Tell it a time *before* the time you told the VCR, then tell it to go off *after* the time you told the VCR to go off. Do this by pushing 'Channel.'

"We're almost home now. You have to understand, for these machines to work, they have to be turned off before they're turned on. For them *not* to work, they have to be left on. So never leave your converter box on, unless you've turned it off, and always leave your VCR off so that it will come on. Is that clear?

"Perfectly," I said.

"That's about it," he said. "If you any questions, you can ask for me personally. My name's 4-1-9."

Now, the only one who seemed to understand all this was Tucker. That's because, being young and "visual", he did not think "linearly." Whenever a particularly good dog show came on—say a commercial in which a talking parakeet tries to persuade a cat to eat canned cat food instead of live birds—he would jump up, pummel the set and trigger the VCR's "Play" button.

Suddenly, instead of cats and parakeets, we'd be watching Bette Davis blowing smoke at Paul Henreid in *Now Voyager*.

With the technological know-how endogenous to his generation, Tucker would then slam his paw down on "Rewind," causing Bette and Paul to re-inhale, and soon we were back with the cat and the parakeet. It made for a most creative montage.

To us, it was all pretty confusing, but Tucker saw connections we didn't. I'd say he was a kind of electronic Jackson Pollock. He wasn't locked into outmoded concepts, like plot and character. His brain had been wired to McLuhanesque perfection.

I think perhaps in Tucker we saw one of the great leaps forward in Earth's evolution. It won't be completed in our lifetime, of course, but in some future millennium Tucker's descendents will be as at home with electronic gadgetry as today's gradeschoolers are with computers. I can tell you this: By the time he was five Tucker preferred watching Bugs Bunny to chasing real rabbits.

I have no doubt that the networks will soon adjust to this phenomenon and start to create programming for dogs. Knowing that they can feed dogs all the mindless violence they want, programmers will run endless hunt-and-chase scenes, comfortable in the knowledge that the dogs' owners will be too busy or too guilt-ridden to monitor their animals' viewing habits. The only hope may be the D-Chip—the chip the FCC has long been promising to block out dog programs.

If these prognostications are correct, Fox TV, or the next era's equivalent of Fox, will figure out that they can run a day's worth of dog programming for a fraction of what it costs to run Glenn Beck. Which would be a blessing for everyone. All they'll need are some slave-wage Yorkies and a camera on a roller-skate.

From there, it will be but a short hop until some future Ted Turner announces that he has started The Doggie Channel, featuring endless squirrel chases through knee-high swamp grass with halftimes hosted by Benji. Critics, of course, will complain about the exclusion of other species, so they'll throw in a couple of Garfield cartoons under "public interest programming."

We humans might find all this appalling, but our dogs will remind us that we didn't appreciate MTV when it first came out either. Some of us still don't. But the dogs of the future will be every bit as savvy, and probably as stubborn, as today's pre-teen humans. As the evening wears on, we'll tell them, "Turn off that set!" We might even demand that they do something constructive with their time, like surfing the Internet.

"Aw, heck!" they'll bark. "The Net's so *slow!*"

"Okay, pup," we'll say. "It's into the tub with you!"

Sag Harbor and the Movies

Since we never learned how to operate our VCR, we often have to get in a car and actually go out to a movie.

Movie-going on the East End is very popular—so much so that East Hampton has its own film festival and Sag Harbor's art theatre continues to survive even in an age of Adam Sandler.

But there's a peculiar thing about these theatres. Although most are part of the United Artists chain (an exception being Sag Harbor), they don't show the same shows. And the shows they do show seem to be demographically biased for reasons not clearly understood.

For example, if the movie is good and stars Meryl Streep, it will play in East Hampton. If the film is lousy and stars Bruce Willis, it will play in Southampton. If the show has both Meryl Streep and Bruce Willis, it will play in Hampton Bays.

Why this is so, I don't know, but it means that if you live in Water Mill, as I do, you have to put a lot of miles on your car in order to see an intelligent movie.

But let's talk about the Sag Harbor movies. Those are really interesting. In fact, Sag Harbor is interesting, so let's talk about that.

Sag Harbor is unquestionably the most self-absorbed and self-referential community on the East End. The people who live there don't know or care about anyone who does not live in Sag Harbor. Moreover, they think that those who do not live in Sag Harbor should be as interested in Sag Harbor as they are.

It's the only village that has its own newspaper, its own mayor, its own police department, and its own library, all at once. If a Sag Harborite asks you, "Who won the election?" he is not talking about a town or national election. He is talking about a *Sag Harbor* election, which to him is more important than who won the World Series.

There is a popular store in Sag Harbor called Provisions. It's a little mom-and-pop place (with mostly organic food, of course) that has both a grocery department and a restaurant. If a Sag Harborite says he'll meet you there, you'll have to understand what that means.

You see, there are two doors to Provisions, and if you don't know which door to use, you're in trouble.

That happened to me once. I stood waiting at the front door for a half-hour while my appointment was waiting at the side door. When we finally made contact, he expressed bewilderment at my stupidity. Every Sag Harborite knows that if you're going to have lunch at Provisions you enter through the side door and you only use the front door if you're going to buy groceries. It never occurred to him that I would be so ignorant.

Sag Harbor also has the East End's neatest five-and-dime store, the most picturesque hotel, the most interesting (but not necessarily friendliest) hardware store, and the best live theatre (the Bay Street Theatre). But we were talking about movies.

The Sag Harbor Theatre is one of those throwbacks to a time when movies weren't called cineplexes. Believe it or not, the Sag Harbor Theatre has only one screen. This can make movie going a bit of a challenge. The theatre often shows three or four movies at the same time—one starting at 4, one at 6, and so on. These movies are inevitably on the effete side and star people like Gwynneth Paltrow in a drama where nobody swears.

I don't particularly like effete movies, but I like them better than Adam Sandler movies or movies where people swear. I also like them better than movies where people get blown out of skyscrapers, which are the ones that are shown in Southampton and star Bruce Willis.

In movies with Gwynneth Paltrow, no one gets blown out of skyscrapers, although they may occasionally bare their nipples. That's so the movie will get an R rating and attract young people, who would otherwise never go to see a movie with Gwynneth Paltrow where nobody swears. They get Gwynneth's nipples as a kind of, well, booby prize.

Sitting through one of these movies (and what a marvelous smell the Sag Harbor Theatre has! Sort of like one of your favorite old socks!) can make one long for the days when movies starred women like Claire Trevor and Gloria Graham. Who were Claire Trevor and Gloria Graham? you ask. They were women so tough they could only be tamed by men like Lawrence Tierney and Scott Brady. Who were Lawrence Tierney and Scott Brady? you ask. A couple of B-movie baddies and real-life brothers who were even tougher than Lee Marvin and Richard Basehart.

Lawrence Tierney was so tough he once strangled a man for no reason in *Born to Kill* (1947), and Scott Brady was so tough he took on a psychotic Richard Basehart in *He Walked By Night* (1948). Scott seemed to enjoy doing this even more than Lee Marvin enjoyed throwing hot coffee in Gloria Graham's face in *The Big Heat* (1950).

Claire Trevor and Gloria Graham were so tough, they could scare Jane Greer. Who was Jane Greer? you ask. She was so tough she managed to kill both Kirk Douglas and Robert Mitchum in the same movie, *Out of the Past* (1947), which is not to be confused with *Out of the Fog* (1941), where Ida Lupino was tougher than Claire Trevor.

I don't know why there's so much nudity and swearing in today's movies, but I do know they aren't any tougher. You think Clint Eastwood is tough? Clint Eastwood is a wimp. You want tough, you watch Laird Cregar threatening Victor Mature in *I Wake Up Screaming* (1941), although Cregar was a wuss compared with Richard Widmark threatening Victor Mature in *Kiss of Death* (1947). Richard Widmark was also tough in *Road House* (1948), but there he had to contend with Ida Lupino, who was tougher than Claire Trevor.

They only show these movies on television now at four in the morning. At eight in the evening, they show movies where people swear and get blown out of skyscrapers. That's because the kids are up at eight, and they want to hear people swear while getting blown out of skyscrapers. Unless of course they can get Gwyneth Paltrow's nipples. That's their booby prize.

Dorian Gray's Prostate

While we're on the subject of movies, I have an idea for a screenplay. It's about my prostate.

First of all, you should know that I happen to be possessed of certain genes that make me appear to be somewhat younger than I am. This is owing mainly to my hair, which over the years has not appreciably thinned or grayed.

However, I am no more immortal than anyone else, as proof of which I will point, at least figuratively, to my prostate.

If Hollywood were to make a movie about my prostate—and

I see no reason why they shouldn't—I think it might be along the lines of the 1945 classic, *The Picture of Dorian Gray*. That's the one based on the Oscar Wilde story about the man who remains young while his portrait ages.

As I imagine it, this movie would take place in a Water Mill castle where a young and irresistibly handsome newspaper columnist makes a pact with the devil to sacrifice his prostate in order to keep his hair.

As time passes, he continues to look youthful while his prostate ages. Not wanting anyone to know, he removes his prostate and takes it to the attic, where he keeps it under lock and key.

When he subsequently marries, he tells his bride, "Now, whatever you do, don't go near that attic."

Of course you know what's going to happen. The first thing women do when told not to do something is to do it. The gods had the same problem with Pandora.

So as soon as the wife thinks her husband is safely out of the way (he's gone to the hardware store, which usually occupies huge chunks of his time) she dons a negligee, lights a candle and goes to the attic.

Now, why all women have to put on negligees and light candles in order to visit creepy parts of a castle is beyond me, but that's what they do. Ask any film director. Even if they have a drawer full of overalls and the house is fully electrified, they have to put on negligees and light their way with candles.

She climbs the long and creaky staircase, and when she arrives at the locked door, she forces it open with a nail file.

This is another strange convention. The castle is full of tools more appropriate for breaking locks—pry bars, screwdrivers, electric drills, sledgehammers—but women always use nail files. What's even more amazing, they work.

The attic is a strange and forbidding place. It has cobwebs all over and a few skeletons which may or may not belong to some ex-wives the husband forgot to mention.

But what attracts her most is the huge, misshapen thing in the corner. It stands alone and is covered with a sheet.

As she approaches, who should be coming home downstairs but her whack-job of a husband, who has failed to find the sandpaper he was looking for and returned early.

He notices that a candle and a negligee are missing from the bedroom and goes to the attic to investigate.

While the violins screech menacingly, the wife approaches the sheet. At the same time, the husband is climbing the stairs. (Admit it, the suspense is killing you!)

Finally, just as she's about to pull off the sheet, he enters and cries, "I warned you! You want to look? Go ahead—look!" and whips off the sheet so that she can see.

The camera zooms in on the prostate, which, to the audience's horror, is the size of a bowling ball and shaped like a baked potato. The wife screams hysterically.

The husband, following another of Hollywood's timeworn traditions, decides now would be a good time to strangle his wife, but just at that moment a young urologist (who has been hanging about ineffectually since the beginning of the story) happens to pass and hear the woman's screams. He rushes in, cries, "Unhand that maiden!" and shoots the husband, killing him.

As the camera cuts to the husband's face, we see his beautiful hair turn white and fall out like everyone else's, while in the corner the prostate returns to its youthful state, looking for all the world like a gland you might find in, oh, say, Ewan McGregor.

The candle ignites the sheet, the castle burns to the ground and the wife runs off with the urologist.

Now, tell me, is that a great story or what? Mr. Spielberg, if you want to reach me, I'm in the book.

Quadrupeds of Domesticity

One day a letter appeared in The *Southampton Press* scolding it for using the phrase "hatchet job." They had used it in a headline involving town politics and the writer thought our Shinnecock neighbors would be upset, since "hatchet job" might refer to scalping somebody.

I cut the letter out and read it to Tucker, thinking he would find it as amusing as I did. He did not.

"Actually," he said, "you've been pretty insensitive yourself lately."

"Really?" I said. "How so?"

As any Westie owner knows, these dogs have no esteem problems. You don't have to tell them how great they are because they already know it. But according to Tucker, I had been using words that wounded his ego.

"Take the word 'dog'," he said, yapping into my computer with bark-recognition capabilities. "You keep using it despite its insulting connotation. 'Low-down dog'. . .'Capitalist running dog'. . . It's a terrible word, and I cry myself to sleep over it."

"I had no idea," I said.

"There's a lot you don't know. Instead of 'dog', I'd prefer to be called a 'quadruped.' I know you humans like to use the D word, but it's time you moved to a higher plane."

Tucker pointed out that even "quadruped" wasn't ideal. He'd prefer "quadruped of domesticity", sort of like the shoe clerk who wants to be called an "executive footwear sales associate."

I asked if there was anything else I should change.

"Yes," he said. "Don't say you're my 'master'. That term went

Ambulatory Assignment of an Olfactory and Evacuative Nature

out with Spot and Rover. I value your judgment, but it requires no elitism. From now on, you're my 'mentor.'"

"Really?" I said.

" Yes. 'Mentor' or 'colleague.' But 'mentor' is better because it has a nicer ring to it. It gives me the feeling of moving up. We all know that mentors are due to retire someday."

"So from now on the two of us are pet and mentor," I said.

"Not pet!" he snapped. "Just because I'm small and lack your upper-body strength does not give you the right to pin diminutives on me."

"So what are you then?"

"I'm your 'canine associate,'" he said. "'Associate and mentor'—that's much more dignified. And we don't go on 'walks,' we go on 'ambulatory assignments of an olfactory and evacuative nature.'"

"Is it all right if I still call cats 'cats'?" I asked.

"No," he snarled. "That's too good for them. 'Cat-like moves'... 'the eyes of a cat'... It's enough to make you sick."

"Then what should I call them?" I asked.

"Call them dogs," he said. "Let's see how they like it. When you see a cat, shout, 'You low-down running dog!' That'll teach 'em. They think they're so cool."

"You seem to have a lot of complaints," I said.

"No more than usual. But there are some other things your species has been getting away with for years, like what you call our females. I can't repeat it, but you and I know it's a dirty word, and we never did anything to deserve it."

"You're right," I said. "I'm ashamed just thinking about it."

"These are man's best friends we're talking about. That you and your kind should heap such abuse on us does not speak well for your sense of gratitude."

"So what should we call your females—'quadrupedettes'?" I wondered.

"Stow that!" he snapped. "Spare us your arrogance, buster. Our females want to be treated as equals. Most would prefer to be called 'quadrupersons.'"

"I've got to tell you, this is pretty confusing," I said. "We've been using those terms for a lot of years."

"Sure," he snarled. "That's because you're speaking a DWEH language."

"DWEH?" I asked.

"Dead White European Human," he said.

Dog of the Millenium

Unfortunately, Tucker died a few years back, depriving Princeton of one of its best prospects. After an appropriate period of grief, we decided to get another Westie.

Here I must say that trying to replace one dog with another doesn't always work out. While there are similarities within a breed, each animal is different, and that certainly pertains to Westies.

We named this new puppy MacDuff and explained to him what a great tradition he was coming from. After all, Tucker had been accepted by Princeton.

This did not go over. Not long after bringing him home, I heard my wife say, "MacDuff, literature is to be respected, not chewed." She was saying that while trying to get a copy of George Eliot's *Middlemarch* out of MacDuff's mouth.

As I've explained, Tucker was a Dog of the Nineties, modern for his time but outmoded when the calendar reached 2000. MacDuff is a Dog of the Millennium. That means in his eyes, Tucker was a dweeb.

In fact, I heard him say exactly that as my wife tried to get the book out of his mouth. "As a Dog of the Millennium, I decry out-of-date linear media," he said. "If you want to reach me, try Facebook."

He also said that Dogs of the Millenium know that Wolf Blitzer is not in that box. "We know Wolf Blitzer is an alien cyborg beamed down from Mars," he said. "If you watched *The X-Files*, you'd know that."

"But why do you chew books?" my wife asked.

"Because, as a Dog of the Millennium I am not just visual, but hyper visual. George Eliot is not hyper visual. I have been tearing the pages out of this book for the past hour and haven't come across a single squirrel chase."

"I don't think George Eliot was interested in chasing squirrels," my wife said.

"Some chick goes around calling herself George," he said, "who knows what she's interested in."

Actually, MacDuff has some virtues Tucker didn't. I often felt Tucker would have come up with $E=MC^2$ had he just lived long enough. MacDuff lacks that capacity, but he is good at interpersonal relationships. Think of him as the George W. Bush of dogs.

If other dogs are grouchy, MacDuff knows how to cheer them up. He bounces around, sniffs their rear ends, then humps their heads. I'm not sure W. did that, but I seem to recall that we did have one recent president for whom head humping was not unusual.

Anyway, what MacDuff *does* do—and do very well—is chew.

"Tell you what," my wife said. "I'll give you two Danielle Steels and a Robert Ludlum in exchange for the *Middlemarch*."

"Junk food," he growled.

"But you don't like George Eliot," she said. "You said you don't. You give me the *Middlemarch* and we'll toss in a couple of William Dean Howellses and James Fenimore Coopers." (I haven't read William Dean Howells and James Fenimore Cooper in years and hope I never have to again.)

"You can't pull that old hostage-negotiation gambit on me," he said. "You give me the William Dean Howells and the James Fenimore Cooper and I'll eat them on top of the *Middlemarch*. Dogs of the Millennium can have it all."

"You can't live in our house," she said, "if you're going to eat our books. We like those books. They contain the wit and wisdom of the ages. What if we give you a copy of *The Wizard of Oz*, and you give me back the *Middlemarch*? There's a little dog in *The Wizard of Oz* who's about your size and with whom you can play till your heart's content."

"I'll wait for the DVD," he said.

"Young dog," she said, "I don't think you've learned to appreciate the deeper things in life. That's the trouble with your generation. You have no understanding of philosophy, of art. Why, there's a whole rich tapestry of existence you haven't even begun to experience yet."

"That's what you think," he said. "Go look at your curtains."

MacDuff Assesses the Animal Shelter

About the only thing that brings out more craziness among people on the East End than school taxes and the Clyde Beatty-Cole Brothers Circus is what does or doesn't go on in the local animal shelter. You see, Southampton has an animal shelter*, and the people who run it are under constant attack from people who think they can run it better. There's no evidence that they *can* run it better, but they are convinced that this shelter is the East End's equivalent of *The Island of Dr. Moreau*.

One day *The Press* ran an article saying that the shelter might have to euthanize some cats or dogs in order to make room for other animals. I thought MacDuff would be interested in this.

I said, "Listen to this, MacDuff. The people at the animal shelter are saying that if a dog can't get with the program, he's toast. What do you think of that?"

Having lived with dogs for some time, I've learned that most of them are Republicans. They love authority, are suspicious of

*Or did. In 2009, it reverted to private ownership because of all the squabbling and backbiting going on. It was also losing money. But none of that makes the slightest difference to MacDuff. Fiduciary matters were never his strength.

change and believe there are no free lunches, unless it's for themselves. But I figured that, at least in this case, he'd be on the side of the bleeding-hearts.

To my surprise, he wasn't. Instead, he said, "That depends. How many of those dogs have peed on smaller dogs' heads?"

Right there I knew we were heading toward the kind of defining moment that took place in the 2000 presidential debates when the moderator asked Al Gore and George W. Bush how they would handle criminals. After Gore gave his usual wonkish reply, Bush responded by saying, "In Texas we know what to do with 'em. We kill 'em."

MacDuff, like President Bush, doesn't do nuance. When I said I didn't know whether any of the doomed dogs were guilty of peeing on smaller dogs' heads, he said, "Well, a lot do, you know. How would you like it if you were standing there minding your own business and a stranger came up and peed on your head?"

I had to admit, I wouldn't like it, but since it had never happened, I thought we were speaking hypothetically.

"*I'm* not," he said. "If a Dalmatian or chow-chow can't control himself, I say give him the needle. That's what a Texan would do."

"But listen to this," I said. "Here's an article that says Pat Lynch*, the writer of so many of these diatribes, has been permanently barred from the shelter because she's a bully and a disruptive influence. Isn't it sad that a woman who's trying to save your comrades' lives is treated like a criminal?"

---

*Another name to reckon with. Pat Lynch is in the business of hounding people in the name of hounds. If a dog is involved, Pat is front and center. For awhile she had a job at *The Press* writing a column called Shelter Stories, but then the town sought a restraining order to keep her away from the shelter. She sued, and eventually won, but it was all quite messy. Anyway, if you are going to say anything good about the animal shelter, or bad about dogs, you'll have to deal with Pat Lynch.

"I don't know," he said. "Some of these dames are kooks. But I can tell you this: Any dog that pees on a smaller dog's head doesn't deserve pity. You bleeding hearts always want to defend the pit bulls. Have you ever been walking along, minding your own business, and suddenly had a pit bull's nose up your rear end?"

"I can't say as I have," I said.

"Well, it's no fun. I've had it happen right on Main Street. I've been standing in front of Hildreth's admiring the legs on their teak benches and suddenly there's a pit bull's nose up my rear. It's disgusting. I turn around and let him have it, both barrels. I say, 'I'm not that kind of dog! Do that again and you lose your snout!'"

"Seems to me I've seen you do the same thing to other dogs," I said.

"Don't change the subject," he said. "I live by the Terrier's Golden Rule."

"What's that?"

"'Better you than me.'"

"Well," I said, "it just seems that death is kind of a draconian solution for a dog that may not have had the advantages you've had."

"Spoken like a true Massachusetts liberal," he said. "It's a dog-eat-dog world out there. You sit here with your fancy newspaper and have no concept of reality. Walk a mile in my paws. See what it's like having to deal with squirrels and chipmunks who are always trying to muscle in on your turf. See what it's like listening to some half-baked cat cry, 'Tee-hee! I can climb trees and you can't!' I tell you, it's tough."

"So you don't care if those poor animals are euthanized," I said.

"Listen, when you've been around as long as I have," he said, "you learn that there's only one dog that counts."

"And I suppose I can guess which one that is," I said.

"Shut up and bring me my lunch," he said.

And About those "No Dogs" Signs...

MacDuff says he is sick and tired of specism on the East End. Be assured that he doesn't like racism or sexism either (well, maybe sexism; male Westies haven't quite "got it" yet), but his main concern is specism. He believes it is evil and must be stopped.

MacDuff says that when he goes to JFK Airport in Queens, he finds no signs forbidding him from entering. Dogs are usually treated well at JFK, pampered by kind-hearted stewardesses who have just come off long trans-oceanic flights and can't wait to see their own pets back home.* MacDuff likes that.

But when he goes to Macarthur Airport in Islip, he is immediately confronted by insulting signs forbidding him from entering the terminal unless he's caged. These signs say nothing about snakes, squirrels, gnus or hamsters—they pointedly and outrageously single out dogs.

Here in Water Mill, we have the friendliest post office in the world, yet the sign on the door baldly states "NO DOGS ALLOWED (Except Seeing Eye Dogs)." MacDuff points out that he has not bitten a mailman in years (although that may be because our mail is delivered by truck). He wants a law making it

*At least that used to be the case. Lately, JFK has become meaner, no doubt because of such things as the shoe bomber and the Christmas bomber. Now they seem to view all four-footed creatures as agents of Osama bin Laden.

illegal for government institutions to discriminate against anything on the basis of race, sex, creed or species. (He is willing to exempt cats. Cats, he points out, are often undocumented.)

The experiences he's had are humiliating. One summer we went to Montauk State Park, where, when we pulled into the parking lot, we were stopped by a rude sign and an equally rude attendant. Both said, "No dogs!"

"But this is a public park!" I said. "MacDuff wants to see the lighthouse."

"No dogs!" the attendant repeated, and she glowered at MacDuff through the closed car window as if he were a Tasmanian devil. "He's not even allowed to sit in the car here!"

MacDuff could hardly believe his ears. He is seriously considering a lawsuit.

Last year, we took him to Mashomack Preserve on Shelter Island so that he could see the great job the Nature Conservancy is doing there.

"No dogs," they said.

"Just a little minute," I said. "Doesn't the Nature Conservancy protect *all* animals and assure that they survive in the wild?"

"Yes," said the Conservancy man, "but piping plovers don't like dogs, and at Mashomack, plovers rule."

To MacDuff, this was incredible. He pointed out that in a truly free preserve there are always risks, and animals cannot just hide behind quotas. "There are no free lunches in the woods!" he barked. "The whiny plovers have to get over it!"

MacDuff believes that if the plovers can't pull their weight and survive without help, they're due for a little downsizing. (There's a body of opinion that says that the only difference between MacDuff and Pat Buchanan is their voices. MacDuff's is mellower.)

It might be well to remember that dogs are not treated this way in other cultures. In France, dogs wander in and out of restaurants at will. In England, dogs are preferred over children. (At least British dogs. All foreign dogs have rabies.) MacDuff feels that it's up to the enlightened artists and intellectuals of the Hamptons to lead our country out of this morass. As a terrier, he believes there should be no limits on his aspirations and that whatever he wants he should have—instantly.

MacDuff is thinking of asking Paul Simon to take up his cause with a benefit concert. Failing that, he is calling upon all dogs to join him in a pee-in on the Water Mill Village Green. There'll barking, howling and raised-leg protests. That will be followed by Kibbles 'n Bits in the post office lobby.

What Hamptons Birds Want

Besides dogs, cats and horses, the most popular nonaquatic animal on the East End is the bird. The bird comes in various forms and shapes. There are the geese who used to pass through on their way south but who now, like my wife and me, stick around all winter; the ducks that hunters like to shoot at dawn in order to rouse all the weekenders out of their hungover stupors; the egrets that wade around in sanctuaries showing off their legs; the ospreys that, for reasons best known to ospreys, live on top of telephone poles. (How ospreys survived before Alexander Graham Bell invented the telephone is anybody's guess.)

But let's talk about some of our more common birds—our wrens, our finches, our martins. Specifically, what do these birds demand in terms of living accommodations?

I ask this because every spring I put up a bird house and every spring nobody comes. The birds take one look and give it the raspberry. It's most disheartening.

I'll admit, they're just spec bird houses. They weren't designed with any particular customer in mind. I just throw them up, as developers do, in the expectation that there will be plenty of birds who will be thrilled to spend the summer in a little house out here near the beach. I mean, it's got to be better than Brooklyn, right?

Unfortunately, it hasn't worked out that way. Myself, I don't speak Bird, but MacDuff does, so I went to him and asked his opinion.

"Sounds like you don't know your market," he said. "In the bird-house business, it's location, location, location. Where did you hang it?"

"In a tree," I said.

"Try not to sound stupider than you look," he said. "The main reason bird houses go unoccupied is because the builder put them in the wrong place. They either hung them too high or too low. They put them too close to a highly-trafficked area or somewhere where a cat can get at them.

"In this case, I think you hung it too far north," he said. "You're dealing with a bullish market and a demanding generation of bird. These sparrows want to be south of the highway, not up here with the grackles fighting over every potato bug. If I were you, I'd find a nice tree on Further Lane and hang it there. You'd be surprised the response you'll get."

"But I don't own a tree on Further Lane," I said.

"In that case, you'll have to throw in some goodies. What kind of windows does the house have?"

"It doesn't have windows," I said. "I didn't think birds needed windows."

10 Nesting Rooms Plus Worm Cellar (Call for price)

"Ah-ha! Today's bird wants a neo-Victorian shingleside with a wraparound veranda and lots of Palladian windows. All you're giving them is a little hole. How do you think Chuck Scarborough's* wife would feel if all Chuck gave her was a house with a little hole? Tell me about the kitchen."

"I figured they'd do most of their eating out," I said.

"Jeez oh man! Today's bird wants a kitchen with Corian, granite or Florentine marble countertops. No Formica, got it? The little missus wants a microwave, a Garland or Viking stove, and a Sub-Zero for the kiddies to store their beetles. Did you provide a worm cellar?"

"I didn't know birds needed a worm cellar." I said.

"Well they do. Describe the great room to me."

"What's a great room?" I said.

"That's what fogies like you used to call a living room. Is it at least two stories high with a cathedral ceiling and lots of skylights?"

"It doesn't have skylights," I said, "but I guess you'd say it's plenty cathedral."

"Where's the wet bar?"

"I didn't think birds needed wet bars," I said.

"If you want to attract today's bird to a crummy spec house north of the highway where they're going to have to put up with raccoons and God-knows-what-all, you better give 'em a wet bar. How about the pool?"

"I thought they'd just go out and use the sprinkler," I said.

"You mean like some kid in the Bronx? Listen. Today's bird

---

*Chuck Scarborough, the popular New York newscaster, is a longtime East End resident who by all accounts is a regular guy—or was until the Village of Southampton wanted to put a painted bike lane in front of his driveway. At that point, he became somewhat irregular. After he got all of his well-to-do friends to protest, the village pulled in their horns and the bike lanes went elsewhere.

wants his great room to look out over his tennis court and his Gunnite pool. These birds have put in grueling hours and taken enormous risks to get where they are, and they expect rewards."

At that point, I felt pretty discouraged. "You've made it sound so difficult," I said, "I'm not sure I can build a house like that."

"I'm not sure either," he said. "That's why I suggest you call Hamilton Hogue. And when you do, tell him to make sure he hangs it within easy paw's reach for a Westie."

The World's Energy Crisis, Solved!

One of the ongoing issues out here on the East End is energy. Some of you may recall that a while back our local power company, what at that time was called LILCO but now is called LIPA, wanted to build a nuclear power plant in Shoreham. Many Long Islanders were not keen on that. They imagined that we would have some sort of Chernobyl in our backyard, with no way to escape except by kayak. That might have been a bit hysterical, but that's how Long Islanders are.

There has also been a lot of discussion about solar energy and windmills. Some of the town boards, for instance, have suggested that it would be a good idea if everyone used solar energy to heat their swimming pools. That was not greeted too warmly (ha-ha) by the swimming pool industry, but at least it showed a certain progressiveness.

Not so the use of wind turbines. Although windmills have been a trademark of the East End since the first one was built 1697 on Ox Pasture Road, modern wind turbine boosters failed to reckon on the Committee Against Everything.

The Committee Against Everything, which I described back in the footnote to the essay called *The Great Hamptons Clearances*, is opposed to the addition of new windmills just as they are opposed to the removal of *old* windmills. The Committee Against Everything wants everything to remain just as it was on any given day, although which day that is is for them to know and you to find out.

Anyway, I think I have a better idea. A California company called Norcal Waste Management has announced that it plans to use the methane gas in dog poop to power businesses and homes throughout San Francisco.

I mentioned this to MacDuff, and he said, "When do we move?"

MacDuff has long thought his poop has been undervalued. It's the thing he does best, next to chewing, and he'd like to get credit for it.

Every morning he's at our bed scratching and saying, "Hey, let's go out and make more energy!" He had just read where the retired head of Exxon was paid more than $144,000 a day for doing nothing more than sitting at his desk. Surely, he said, a dog deserves at least that much for producing a product that people can actually use.

Our backyard is a veritable storage shed of unutilized energy cells. MacDuff says, "You don't know it, but you're sitting on a goldmine out here." I tell him, "I hope I'm not sitting on it—but I'm afraid I might be stepping in it."

MacDuff believes that because of him, our property has become an enormous source of untapped gas. He compares it with Saudi Arabia. He feels he should get more respect for this and also more Eukanuba, since, after all, what comes out must first go in.

Unfortunately, this raises the question of what exactly does go in, because, you see, I happen to know something about dog food.

True, I know more about dog poop, but I know something about the food as well.

I once knew a veterinarian who owned a dog food company. I also knew an advertising man who represented a large dog food manufacturer. Between them, I learned a great deal.

I learned that one of the things pet food companies do is run tests to find out how much of the product's energy remains inside the dog instead of in the poop. You may not believe this, but some of these companies analyze the poop produced in dog kennels and explode it under highly-controlled laboratory conditions. (Where else can you get information like this?) They have sophisticated meters called poop-o-meters, or something like that, which measure the explosive impact of the poop, with the goal of keeping as much energy inside the dog as possible.

Unfortunately, this research runs counter to the needs of us energy consumers. I mean, here's a world hungering for docile, phlegmatic dogs who produce high-octane poop, and instead we're getting rambunctious dogs with lethargic excrement.

In an ideal world, dogs would barely have enough energy to roll over in the morning, while the poop they produce would be dancing the Macarena on our sidewalks.

I'm hoping to correct this oversight and use MacDuff's nutritionally enhanced poop to reduce our gas and electric bills. In the not-to-distant future I'd like to be able to say, "MacDuff, I want to run my table saw today. Go out and make a pile."

He'd go out and do his usual spinning and turning moves (presumably to face whatever Mecca dogs need to face for this function), and I'd pick up the result and scoop it into a large combustion chamber on the side of the house.

There, pistons would fire and the released methane would turn a huge turbine atop our roof.

This would power massive drive belts that in turn would spin the mandrel on my table saw in the basement.

"More poop!" I'd cry, and MacDuff would strain for all he's worth to try to get my saw up to warp speed.

This would enable me to cut kindling for a fire that we'd have that night in order to heat the house while MacDuff eats the Eukanuba he needs to produce more poop the next day. It's what you'd call the perfect self-sustaining ecosystem.

According to a man named Robert Reed, who works for Norcal Waste, a dog's poop, even after the unconscionable tampering of companies like Purina and Science Diet, produces far more energy than cow or sheep dung. As for cats, forget it—they don't produce enough methane to run a nightlight.

But in MacDuff I think we may have the future Exxon. Here he comes now. He's got that look. Stand back, everybody, he's starting to spin…

Hail, Graduates!

One of our great local assets is the confusingly named Southampton College, once named the Southampton Campus of Stony Brook University and before that the Southampton Campus of Long Island University. It's really a very nice school, and if people would stop renaming it and trying to shut it down, it would be even better. But that's not what this essay's about. This essay's about a bone I have to pick.

First, a word about why all the best things on the East End are at constant risk of being shut down. You will note that the worst things out here—the noisy nightclubs, the overpriced restaurants, the illegal group party houses—are never at risk of being shut down. They are like cockroaches—no matter how hard you try, you can't stomp them out. But if it's an art museum, an animal shelter, or a publicly-funded radio station—watch out. At any given time, it will face extinction.

In some cases, I can understand why. There are well-meaning people who are willing to fund the creation of something, but not its maintenance. It's like the politician who wants to take credit for building a bridge but not for painting it. That has been the case with the animal shelter, the Children's Museum in Bridgehampton, and Southampton College.

Southampton College is best known for its marine science program and its creative writing program, which makes it all the more inexplicable that they have never asked me to give their commencement address. I mean, aren't colleges supposed to give kids role models to look up to? Who would be better than a famous *Southampton Press* columnist?

Well, you will be relieved to hear that I have a speech all lined up should they ever come to their senses and ask me. Here it is:

> Alumni, Administrators, Faculty, Eager Members of this Graduating Class:
>
> I can't tell you what an honor it is to be here today. This weekend, not only here, but in colleges and universities all over the country, students are being reminded that, in this complex world of strife and turmoil, one lone person *can* make a difference.
>
> As you leave here today, I would remind you of that, too. I would also fervently beg that you not be the one.
>
> Don't take that too hard. If everyone went out and made a difference, think of what a mess we'd be in. Immanuel Kant said that we should never do anything with-

out considering what would happen if our actions became a universal law. It's one thing for you to go out and be the one who makes a difference, but what about that jerk sitting next to you? Face it, that guy's a world-class loser. We'd all be better off if he's lost in the shuffle.

For all we know, Adolph Hitler got his start by being urged to be the one who makes a difference. His mother wanted him to open a bed-and-breakfast. "You have such a way with strudel!" she told him. "I beg of you, Adie, don't exert yourself!"

But would he listen? No. Some fool of a commencement speaker told him to be the one who makes a difference, and look what happened.

At this very moment, tomorrow's Charles Mansons, Osama bin Ladens and Saddam Husseins are sitting in commencement ceremonies being told that they should go out and be the one who makes a difference. *Oy vai!* What's wrong with this proposition is that it's assumed they'll know what difference the world wants them to make. Even in America, every four years the majority of voters tell the losing candidate they don't like the difference he's made. Nobody likes people who make a difference. What they like are people with crinkly smile lines.

Another thing commencement speakers tell you is that you should "assume the mantle of leadership." Ha! You'll note that the guy telling you that is the kind who likes to wear such mantles himself. He is not about to hand over anything to the likes of you. Make no mistake: He does not intend for you to lead until he's darn well ready to let you. You try to assume his mantle and you're looking for a punch in the snoot.

While we're talking leadership, consider the fact that if you all become leaders, there will be nobody to follow. Would it make sense for a speaker to stand in front of the graduating class of the Juilliard School of Music and tell them all to go out and become leaders? The tubas? The timpanis? The viola de gambas? I'd hate to hear what they'd sound like. "Go forth and don't make a peep," I'd tell them, "until I've told you to."

I don't think you should all go out and "get involved," either. That's another thing speakers always tell you. This very weekend, every airhead with a mortar board is being told to go out and "get involved." For Pete's sake, why? I'd like you to consider the possibility that the reason this world is in such a mess is because too many people have gotten involved in it. There's been an obvious overabundance of chiefs and not enough Indians. If we're talking politics (and, this being a commencement, what else would we be talking?), I'd suggest that getting involved is second only to religious fanaticism as a way of making everyone miserable.

Eager graduates, in my opinion, the man who most closely had it right was Francois Marie Arouet, better known as Voltaire. He said that if you are going to do your best in this best of all possible worlds, you should just tend your own garden. That makes sense. Years from now, when you have nothing to show for it but being third runner-up in a Stern's Miracle-Gro contest, then you can go out and make a difference. By then, I hope I'm not around to see it.

Gardening on the East End

Did someone mention gardening? Well, gardening is an important component of East End life, and over the years, my column has made every effort to quench readers' thirst in this area.

Some time ago, a Water Mill neighbor who happens to be a

farmer (and a descendent of one of the original settlers) wrote a letter to the editor complaining about a proposed policy that would prevent local farm stand owners from harvesting their crops without a town building inspector's prior approval. He seemed to think that his family, which had been farming out here since 1640, knew more about crops than a Southampton building inspector.

I begged to differ. While I have not been here since 1640, I own a raised vegetable garden, and I need all the help I can get.

I am particularly hopeful that the building inspector can tell me what's wrong with my lima beans. Every year I try to grow lima beans, and every year they curl up and die.

This causes great hardship for my family. Store-bought limas are expensive, and it would be wonderful if my wife and I could enjoy bountiful beans for the price of a Burpee packet.

But every year our good cheer fades as, one by one, the plants turn black and keel over.

Unlike my neighbor, I have great faith in our building department's ability to solve such problems. Upon reading of their new role in agriculture, I called and asked if they would come look at my limas. "Maybe I'm putting too much captan in them," I said. "Or maybe I'm not supposed to put any in."

The woman who answered didn't seem to understand. "We don't have any captains in this department," she told me.

Granted, I may have been watching too many Miracle-Gro commercials, but it was obvious that my garden needs stricter controls. "Your department's got their noses into everything else," I told her. "No reason they shouldn't be into my lima beans, too."

While they're at it, they should also look at my radishes. Every year, spurred by a fatal combination of overconfidence and impatience, I jump the gun and pull up my radishes before their time. Seeing those little green shoots sticking up out of the ground, I think they're ready to go and feel profoundly disappointed when there's nothing on the other end but inedible pustules.

My wife gets furious. She says, "From now on, I don't want you to touch a single radish until the building inspector says you can!"

I told the building department spokeswoman that their inspectors had done a wonderful job with our swimming pool. "We put in a pool a few years ago," I told her, "and your inspector came and said, 'Well, you can have the pool, but you can't put chairs around it.'"

It seems our plan to surround the pool with on-grade flagstones constituted what he thought was a "nonconforming structure."

"You mean," I said, "I can have mud around my pool, but I can't have stones to put chairs on?"

"That's right," he said. "People can run out to your pool, jump in, and run back again, but they aren't allowed to sit around it. If you insist on laying stones out there, when you go to sell your house we'll make you pick them all up and stack them in your yard, and the guy who buys it will have to put them all back again."

Yessir, that's the kind of man I want regulating my lima beans.

I believe that the building department is every bit as qualified to be crop inspectors as they are to be building inspectors. Conversely, I think they should consider turning over their building inspections to the Cornell Agricultural Extension. Cornell would have more sense regarding our swimming pool.

Anyway, I can see those building department guys now, running around in their Day-Glo vehicles, red lights flashing, sirens screaming, rushing to a Corwith or Zaluski farm field to see if the tomatoes are ready to be picked. And woe be to those whose fruit is still green! We aren't just talking significant financial penalties; the man who vetoed my poolside flagstones will make them take those tomatoes and glue them back on the vines.

No, with all due respect to my neighbor, I welcome the building department's interest. In fact, I think maybe we should get the fire and police departments involved, too.

Dog Days in the Garden

Of course I always start off thinking that this year I'll have a really great garden and won't need anybody's help. In May, as I put the seeds in the ground, the future looks brilliant. But as the summer wears on and the gardening chores begin to pall, my optimism fades and I realize that I've made the same old mess I made last year and the year before.

I neglected my early herbicide applications, so now there's more crabgrass than grass. I put off pruning the shrubs, and now I can hardly get up the front walk.

The pines in the backyard need trimming, and the locust trees, which I've been fighting for 25 years, have shot up another generation of Kryptonite-resistant cyborgs.*

---

*Locust trees are the botanical equivalent of cockroaches. They grow on runners, spring up everywhere and are virtually impossible to destroy. Think of the sci-fi classic *The Day of the Triffids* crossed with *Little Shop of Horrors*, and you'll have some idea of what I'm up against.

This means I have to go through the same struggles I did last year, even though these are the days when I'd rather be lying in a hammock.

The first order of business is to bring out the old chainsaw. That's always fun. I hate chainsaws. Not because they're scary, but because they're so inconvenient.

Locust trees being as hard as concrete, the blades on a chainsaw will only last about 10 minutes while trying to fell one. And replacing a chainsaw blade is one of the more frustrating chores in life.

In the first place, the blades are always filled with grease and gunk, so you get oil and sap all over. If you don't wear gloves, you'll probably cut off something you'll wish you hadn't.

The replacement process requires the training of a surgeon. Why can't they make chainsaws like Gillette razors? Why can't they make them so you just go push-pull, click-click and the old blade drops off and a new one snaps on?

First you have to unscrew some lug nuts, then you have to take the case apart. After that, you have to take the old blade off and try to put the new one on with its teeth pointing the right way. I always mess that up.

Finally, you have to use a screwdriver, a wrench and three pairs of hands to get the right tension.

I suppose if I were a professional I'd be able to do it in my sleep. It would be like field-stripping that old M-1 the Army once issued me. But since I don't saw things for a living, I always get something wrong. That means that when I go to start the engine the chain flies off and I become my own Texas Chainsaw Massacre.

Then there are the lawn chemicals. Listen, I'm a big supporter of Group for the East End, and I've read with dismay what lawn chemicals do to our bays and ponds. But I am determined to have this tiny sward I call my yard look as verdant as possible, so too bad. We all have our vices. Some people smoke.

So I get out the fertilizers and the weed killers and I read what I'm supposed to do, which itself requires a PhD in chemistry.

Under DIRECTIONS FOR USE, there are no directions for use—just warnings. These come from the FBI, the FDA, the DEA and the USDA. They tell you that if you screw up and apply this stuff wrong, it's off to Guantánamo with you.

When you finally get to what you're supposed to do, you find there are so many preconditions you might as well give up. Maybe you were supposed to have sprinkled first and didn't. Maybe you were not supposed to have sprinkled first and did.

Maybe you can't put the chemical down if it's going to rain within 48 hours, or maybe it has to rain within 48 hours for the stuff to work. It requires a short course in meteorology.

Then there's the measuring challenge. The directions say "3 tbs per gallon", only the bottle is in milliliters and the applicator is in ounces. You need a laboratory full of beakers and converter charts to figure it out.

When finally you go to apply the stuff, you find that your hose is too short. But that's all right, because your hose-end applicator doesn't work anyway. You forgot to clean it after last year.

Your hand-held sprayer has a leak in it, you can't use your wife's watering can lest the residue kill every plant in the house, and if the chemical is granular, the bag gives you settings for every spreader known to man except the one you own.

By this time, you can't wait for fall. In recognition of which, this poem:

A Gardener's Prayer

I know I should be diffident,
But this year will be different;
My garden will be too sublime for words.
My string beans will be yummy,
My rhubarb won't be gummy,
My berries won't get eaten by the birds.

These early days in Maytime,
A full-of-hope and gay time,
When nothing bad has undermined my toil,
I find I'm optimistic
That nothing will get cystic
And things will spring like topsy from the soil.

For when it's planting season
I lose all sense and reason
And dream of produce dripping from the vine.
My roses won't get beetles,
My thistles won't have needles,
The nectar from my grapes will taste like wine.

It's with such rosy pictures,
Devoid of any strictures,
That now I plant my seedlings in the ground.
I'm full of faith and credence
That I have God's allegiance
And everything will turn out safe and sound.

Oh, what an annual folly
To be so sure and jolly
And fail to see the serpent lurking near;
For in this world of weedin'
There is no surefire Eden,
And everything I do will end in tears.

The first grim sign of trouble,
Exploding my frail bubble,
Is when the beans I sowed don't show their heads.
It seems the nights grew coldish,
Which made the subsoil moldish,
And now the sprouts have rotted in their beds.

And then comes still more evil
As cutworm, mite and weevil
Begin to eat at blossom, leaf and stem;
And though my heart's organic,
My brain grows wildly frantic,
Compelling me to drastic stratagem.

I rush to garden center,
Consult a helpful mentor,
And load my car with pesticides and sprays;
I bury the requirement
To nurture the environment
And spread those violent poisons in a haze.

Oh, yes, I feel remorseful,
I should be more resourceful,
For cures like these are anodynes at best;

But chemicals are quicker,
Their packaging is slicker,
And I'm dead set on ridding every pest.

I stalk like some grim reaper
Destroying every creeper
And spreading mists of poison through the air;
It's as the purists dreaded,
My kids'll be two-headed,
But frankly at this juncture I don't care.

Despite my violent measures
The bugs will get my treasures
And blight will tear at every stem and leaf;
My lettuce will be bolting,
My peas will look revolting,
And something's sure to bring my kale to grief.

My jalapeño peppers
Will look like dying lepers,
My lawn will fill with mallow, wort and thatch.
The deer will get more savage
And lead the voles to cabbage,
While moles will undermine my peony patch.

And now my tough zucchinis,
Which I had thought Houdinis,
So sly were they at cheating ill and death,
Will emulate my hosta
By giving up the ghosta,
And soon there will be naught but compost left.

I'll lose all my potatoes
As well as my tomatoes,
My broccoli plants will tangle up with weeds;
And further to embarrass us
I'll trample my asparagus,
Which by this time of year has turned to seeds.

I know I should be diffident,
But *next* year will be different;
I won't by Nature's hand be so harassed;
Though if the truth be known
I'm not too good at growin',
And every year turns out much like the last.

Percy Bysshe Shelley, eat your heart out.

When Good Bambis Go Bad

And Furthermore...

When *The Press* first started running my column, the editor asked me what I'd like to call it. I had no idea, so he chose the title *The View East*, and that's what it's been ever since.

But sometimes I've had reason to regret that. My mind refuses to stay focused toward the east or any other direction, and we might have been better off calling it *The View Every Which Way*.

What follows are columns I don't know what to do with. I mean, they aren't really about the Hamptons, but they were conceived on the East End and appeared on the East End, so it would be a shame to not to include them in a book about the East End, don't you agree? Besides, you've spent good money for this opus, and I wouldn't want you to feel cheated.

The two most common questions I hear from New York City people are: 1. What do you do with your time out there in the Hamptons all year? and 2. Where do you come up with your ideas? Of course, the two are related.

The reason New Yorkers can't understand what people do out here all year is because they can't conceive of an existence that depends upon amusing oneself. A New Yorker's life revolves around having things done for him: sitting in a restaurant and having food brought or sitting in a theatre and having a show performed. What his life does not revolve around is amusing himself.

Yet it's precisely because of my ability to do this that the second question poses no problem. For when you aren't depending on other people to amuse you, you have to amuse yourself.

I credit my facility in this area to the fact that I was an only child. Having no brothers or sisters to taunt me, I spent long hours in deep and gratifying conversation with myself. As my wife can tell you, I still do this. During the summer, it is not unusual to see me riding back and forth on my riding mower haranguing some invisible opponent while I cut the grass. During the winter, I do the same thing while shoveling snow. What is more, I invariably win these arguments. You see, having an opponent who's invisible gives you a great advantage. He only puts forth the arguments you want him to.

It also helps to have insomnia. At three in the morning, I'm often lying awake obsessing over things other people would consider trivial. It might be something someone said at a dinner party (see *Women Are From... You Know*) or how annoying sports writers are (see *Dodson's Inferno*), but it's almost always something people in New York rarely think about. People in New York just think about who they're going to sue.

So here are some columns which don't properly fit under any heading, but which I've decided to include anyway. Think of them as added value.

Where My Ideas Come From

One day, my sister-in-law, who was visiting from Washington, suggested that I write a column about packaging. "I bet if you took a poll of East End women," she said, "you'd find that packaging is the most serious thing on their minds."

I must admit, I had not thought of that.

"I agree," said my wife. "Like those Saran Wrap boxes you try to get the wrap out of and they fall apart in your hands because they don't have enough glue on them."

"Or those over-the-counter drugs," said my sister-in-law, "that come in a box the size of a video cassette, but when you get them home you find there are only four pills in there and they're sealed in something so tough you have to use your teeth to get them out."

"Or the milk cartons," said my wife, "that leak all over the fridge but whose tops have all the glue they should have used on the Saran Wrap boxes so you have to try to hack them open with poultry shears and you end up cutting your hand and having to go to the emergency room."

"What about the price tags," said my sister-in-law, "that they put on with Krazy Glue so that you can't get them off even with a razor blade and you have to throw the product away before you've even used it?"

"Or the stickers," said my wife, "that they put on top of the product's seam so that when you go to pull the lid off the tag drops down and you have to use a pair of ice-tongs to fish it out."

"Or the Band-Aids," said my sister-in-law, "that you can't get the wrapper off even though you're bleeding to death, so your bathroom ends up looking like the shower scene in *Psycho* and you have to go to the emergency room."

"Or the FedEx packs," said my wife, "that say, 'tear here" but you can't tear there because it comes off in your hand and there's no way to open it but with a blow torch or a band saw."

"Or the sardine cans," said my sister-in-law, "that tear crookedly along the lid and the key comes off in your hand and you have to open it with a can opener but it's too small and the edge cuts your thumb and you have to wrap your hand in a towel—"

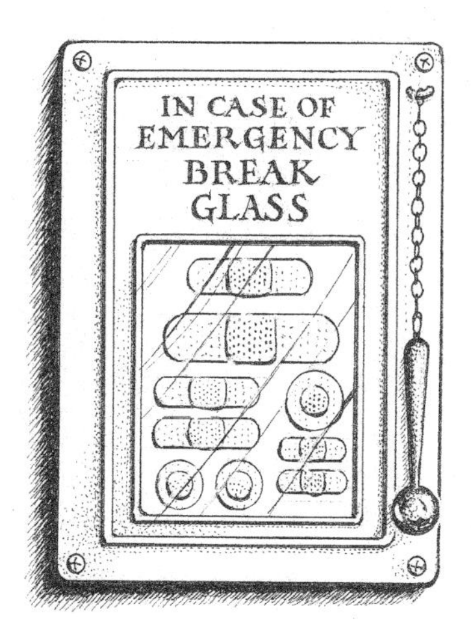

"—because you can't get the Band-Aid wrapper off the Band-Aid—"

"—and go to the emergency room and have stitches put in."

This prompted me to ask about soup cans.

"Soup cans!" cried my sister-in-law. "Don't talk to me about soup cans!"

"Soup cans!" screamed my wife. "*You* try to open a soup can! The can's too small and the magnet doesn't work on your electric can-opener and the can drops off on the floor and the soup flies out and you have to get a new kitchen—"

"—or the lid falls in," said my sister-in-law, "and you can't get it out of the can, and there's this little sharp thingy and you cut yourself and have to go to the emergency room—"

"—because you couldn't get the Band-Aid out of the wrapper—"

"—which is like the cereal boxes that say 'open here' but you can't open them there because they've got too much glue—"

"—which they should have used on the Saran Wrap boxes—"

"—and the cellophane bag won't open either and you have to use a hammer and a chisel—"

"—or your husband's band saw—"

"—which is like the child-proof caps where you have to use pliers—"

"—and the pills spill all over—"

"—and your dog gets into the pills—"

"—and you have to take him to the vet—"

"—or to the emergency room—"

"—and redo your bathroom—"

"—then sell your house."

"Yeah!" they agreed. "Write about *that*!"

So I did.

Alarming News!

Like many men, I buy all my finest jewelry at Ace Hardware.* Therefore, I've come to appreciate having a watch that not only tells time but does everything a real man wants a watch to do.

---

*A word about Herrick, the Ace Hardware store that's in Southampton. Herrick may not be the biggest or even the best hardware store on the East End, but, like a French woman, it does the most with what it's got. How many hardware stores do you know whose manager graduated from Harvard? The thing I've always liked about Herrick is that, although its floor space is limited, there are secret basements and attics full of all sorts of weird inventory. Often, having struck out at Water Mill True Value or Tuckahoe Hardware, I'll go to Herrick looking for a particular hook or flange, and when I show it to the salesman, he'll say, "Oh, we have that. Just a minute," and then he disappears down a little hole and soon emerges with the desired item. So Herrick's holds a particularly warm spot in my heart, even when they aren't selling their famous roasted peanuts. They also used to sell watches, although now they don't.

My Timex Ironman Triathlon Shock Resistant Indiglo Chronometer gives me the day and month, the military time (in several time zones), a split-lap stopwatch for swimming and cycling, and a dozen other features that surpass understanding. This watch is guaranteed to a depth of 200 meters, which, if I remember my scuba lessons correctly, is deeper than any human can survive.

It's not that I really need all these things, I just like knowing they're there.

It also has an alarm. It's not a very loud alarm (in fact, I can hardly hear it), but my wife thinks its deafening.

"Stop beeping!" she'll scream, waking me up in the middle of the night to tell me that my watch is beeping. I sleep with earplugs, so I don't know my watch is beeping. I sleep with earplugs because we used to live in New York, near the Meat Packing District, and at 4 in the morning the truck noise was deafening. I just got in the habit of wearing earplugs and never stopped.

Anyway, when she wakes me up, it scares me to death. I'd turn my watch off, but I don't know how.

For that matter, I don't know how I turned it on. I probably did it when I was trying to reset the hour for Daylight Saving Time. I wish they'd do away with Daylight Saving Time. Given the amount of effort it takes to reset my watch, it would be more proper to call it Daylight Wasting Time.

You're saying, "But why don't you just follow the easy directions that came with the watch?" Okay, I'll tell you why.

I can't read the easy directions that came with the watch. They're in Urdu. Also, my wallet has so much junk in it, I don't have room to carry the instructions.

In order to fulfill the simplest functions of my life, I have to carry four credit cards, a driver's license, a social security card, an ATM card, a medical insurance card, a library card, a health club card, a mini-storage electronic gate access card, three frequent flyer cards, two telephone cards, an Allstate Motor Club Roadside Service card, a Blockbuster Video rental card and a partridge in a pear tree. Where do you want me to keep my watch instructions?

My Timex Ironman Triathlon Shock Resistant Indiglo Chronometer has five buttons. One says "Mode" (I don't know what that means), one says "Indiglo," (that's its underwater night-light—in case you have go to the bathroom down there, I guess), and one says "Set." The other two say "Start" and "Lap/Reset." What they're for, I have no idea. My wife suggests that the "Lap/Reset" button may have something to do with Laplanders, but I can't vouch for that.

Trying to change anything can be disastrous. Wanting to turn off my alarm, I'm just as likely to change my "modes" to a form of Tibetan Standard Time that can only be understood by Navy Seals at a depth of 200 meters. When I try to get out of that, I'm likely to end up in a double-split lap-set that says I have 37 seconds left to reach the top of Mount McKinley and nine seconds left for a medium-rare hamburger.

I'm tempted to stop the alarm by destroying the watch completely, but I'm of an age that can remember John Cameron Swayze saying that Timexes can "take a lickin' and keep on tickin'." Remember that? I can even remember the day he strapped a Timex to the propeller of an outboard motor and turned the motor on to show just what a lickin' a Timex could take. Who will ever forget the look on his face when he pulled the propeller out of the tank and found that the watch had completely disappeared?

Anyway, I figure this Timex Ironman Triathlon Shock Resistant Indiglo Chronometer is the Arnold Schwarzenegger of watches. It can't be stopped and it can't be destroyed. Long after I'm dead and gone, it will be going "beep-beep!" every hour on the hour, reminding the world that "For Whom the Bell Tolls" is no longer the question. It's "For Whom the Watch Beeps"—and it beeps for thee.

He Said, She Said

You will notice that a number of these columns have been about my wife—or more precisely, my relationship with same.

This is another notable feature of year-round East End life. Although most of our summer weekenders are single, most of our year-round residents are married, and if you're going to stay out here all year, through hurricanes, nor'easters and Peter Cook's shenanigans, you'd better have a pretty solid relationship.

I'm pleased to say that my wife and I have such a relationship, although that doesn't mean there haven't been snags. For instance, there was the day she ran over our screen door.

Now before you respond to that, you should know that there are two sides to this story, only one of which is correct. Hear me out, then draw your own conclusions.

At our house, we have a sliding screen door that gives out onto a rear deck. Generations of Westies have used this door to exit in pursuit of intruders, both real and imagined, and this has created a certain amount of wear and tear.

One day I decided to re-screen the slider. I had never re-screened a door that large before, but I had my trusty *Reader's Digest Fix-It-Yourself Book* and figured it couldn't be that tough.

I went to Water Mill Lumber and bought the needed supplies. My biggest problem was to find a suitable workspace. The basement seemed too small and I didn't want to do it outside where the dog could get in the way. So I decided to do it in the garage.

As it happened, my wife was going to the hospital that morning. No, she was not sick; she's volunteers there as an interpreter for Hispanic mothers. I figured this was the perfect time to lay the slider out on the garage floor, clamp it the way they show you in the *Fix-It-Yourself Book* and replace the screen.

In the process of doing this, I got an idea. The aluminum frame could stand a fresh coat of paint. I got out some spray paint, put down some newspapers, and applied a few coats. According to the can, it would take about an hour to dry.

I left the frame on the floor and left the garage door open so my wife would see it. My wife knows that I never leave the garage door open without a reason. I am very neat that way. I always tell her to close the garage door, because leaves blow in. It only made sense that she would realize something was up as soon as she saw the open door.

In the meantime, our pool man came. He was coming to do the final vacuuming before sending me his outrageous bill for opening the pool. He parked his truck on one side of the drive and walked around to the pool.

It was then that my wife came home. I caught up with her a little later over lunch.

"I didn't see your car out front," I said, "Where did you park it?"

"In the garage," she said.

I thought about that a moment, then said, "Where did you put the screen door?"

Now let me address these next few words to my male readers. How would you feel if you asked your wife where she had put the screen door and she said she had left it under the car?

Right. That's how I felt, too.

"Oh, I don't think it's too bad," she said. "The screen is narrower than the car, so only one set of wheels rolled over it."

I went out to the garage and found the car sitting on top of what looked like a piece of flotsam you'd see after a tornado has passed through a trailer park.

"I don't understand how you did that," I said. "I left the garage door open so you'd see it."

"I saw the pool man's truck," she said, "and I thought you had left the door open for him. How was I to know you'd leave a screen door on the floor?"

So there you have it. This is a clear case of women doing irresponsible things, then blaming their husbands. I had to spend the next day straightening out the screen door in my shop. But even now my wife insists it was my fault. "If you had put something high in front of it," she says, "like a bicycle, I wouldn't have hit it."

"If I had put something high in front of it," I say, "like a bicycle, we'd have lost the bicycle, too."

I leave it to you, a jury of impartial readers. Who's to blame here, the honest, hardworking husband who's just trying to improve his home, or the negligent, scatterbrained wife who roars into garages without looking to see if there's a screen door on the floor? You can e-mail me your verdict. Unless, of course, you side with her.

Senior Moments

Of course, staying married means growing old together, and, my dark, unthinned hair notwithstanding, this can lead to impasses.

For example, one morning I was having breakfast, and the woman across from me said, "I told you last night, but you've forgotten."

I find that happens more and more nowadays. I'm sitting there having breakfast and the woman sitting across from me says I've forgotten something that happened the night before.

"I haven't forgotten," I say. "If you had told me last night, I would have remembered."

"I *did* tell you," she says, "but you've forgotten. I told you your memory's getting bad. We had a long conversation about it, but you've forgotten."

She and I are having breakfast. She's having melon with a small wedge of lime, and I'm having Cheerios.

"I have *not* forgotten," I say. "Do you know how insulting it is to sit across the table from a woman you've never met and hear that your memory's getting bad?"

"I'm your wife," she says.

"It is distinctly unpleasant to start the day," I say, "by having someone you've never met tell you that you haven't remembered something that never happened. After beer parties, college girls used to forget things that *did* happen, but I'm not a college girl and I haven't been to a beer party."

"I was telling you that your memory's getting bad and it's something you should accept," she says. "I didn't mean it as an insult. It's simply a fact."

"It's damn insulting," I say, "to have a woman you've never met sit across a table from you and tell you you're in the early stages of whaddayacallit."

"What's whaddayacallit?" she says.

"I forget," I say.

"I said your memory's bad and it gets worse after several glasses of wine. When you've had several glasses of wine, you don't remember things."

"I did not have several glasses of wine. I had *two* glasses of wine, and I remember everything."

"Ron, there's an empty bottle of wine on the kitchen counter, which was full yesterday. You drank it. How can you say you had two glasses of wine when you had a whole bottle?"

"My name isn't Ron, it's Ren," I say, "and I only had two glasses of wine because the first two glasses were medicinal. The French drink wine, and despite the fact that they stuff themselves with goose fat, they don't have heart attacks. It's called the French Paradox. You're allowed two glasses to guard against heart attacks. Whatever *additional* glasses of wine I had were only to enjoy the health bestowed on me by the medicinal glasses. If you don't believe me, ask our doctor."

"Who's that?"

"What's-his-name."

"How else can you explain that you don't remember my telling you that your memory's bad?"

"I'd certainly have remembered you telling me that my memory's bad if you'd told me that, but you didn't, so I'd like to change the subject. Where's the milk?"

"You know where it is. If you want milk, get up and get it."

"I know where it *was*," I said, "but it's not there now because you forgot to buy it."

"If I forgot to buy it," she said, "it's because you forgot to remind me to write it down."

"Why do I have to remind you to write it down?"

"Because, if it's not on my list, I can't remember it. But you're changing the subject. After a couple of glasses of wine, you forget everything, and it's getting worse, like your hearing."

"What's wrong with my earring?"

"Not your earring, your *hearing*. I said you ought to go to a doctor and have your hearing checked. It's a well-known fact that older men suffer significant hearing loss and should go to a doctor now and then to have it checked. There's probably a simple device they can stick in your ear that no one will notice."

"People have been telling me to stick things in my ear for years," I say, "and believe me, I've noticed. There's nothing wrong with my hearing. I can hear better now than I ever did. Why is your wristwatch so noisy?"

"I always dreaded that it would end up like this," she says. "I always said, 'I hope we don't end up like one of those old married couples you see who are always bickering and never agreeing over anything.' But now it's happened."

"It has not happened," I say.

"It has too happened," she says.

"It has *not*," I say.

"Oh, *Ron*!" she says.

Your Kitchen's W.M.D.

Speaking of wives and breakfast, here's something you didn't know: According to an article in the January 28, 2004 edition of *The New York Times*, fastidious women (and the fastidious people of this world are all women, aren't they?) are actually *spreading germs* when they clean house and creating more problems than they solve.

Yes! It's what every little boy knows instinctively: Cleanliness is *bad* for you.

Here's what *The Times* said:

"Chuck Gerba, a professor of environmental microbiology at the University of Arizona who has studied bacteria in home kitchens, said that he found that the people who had the cleanest-looking kitchens were often the dirtiest. Because 'clean' people wipe up so much, they often end up spreading bacteria all over the place. The cleanest kitchens, he said, were in the homes of bachelors, who never wiped up and just put their dirty dishes in the sink."

I knew that. I didn't need some smart-aleck from the University of Arizona to tell me that. Having the kind of scientific mind my wife lacks, I've been saying for years that her insistence on making me put my dirty dishes away is bad for my health. By carping on my dirty dishes and nagging me about the state of our toilets (she seems to think that our house's toilets are my exclusive responsibility), she's endangering both our lives, and perhaps those of our neighbors.

If she had the kind of analytical mind I have, she would know that leaving a pizza box on the coffee table from Super

Bowl Sunday to some point beyond Easter is a recommended precaution against Swine Flu. I keep telling her. I say, "Don't touch that! You'll just spread germs!" But she won't listen. By instinct, I know that you should wait until every living thing has stopped moving in that box. It's what's called "bacteria damage control".

This should be good news to all of you men who, like me, are accused of being pigs. Don't just take my word for it—this is *The New York Times* talking. Your house has never been cleaner than when your wife goes for away for a week to visit your mother-in-law. That Hungry Man frozen food debris you left splotched all over the counter. . .that strange-looking stuff you didn't notice running down the cabinets until it spread all over the floor and made your shoes squeak. . .all that is exactly what antisepsis requires and to interfere with it risks an epidemic.

Another thing the article said—and this really put my mind at rest—is that wood cutting boards are more sanitary than plastic ones. I've always said that, as have the French. The French, who know a great deal more about wood cutting blocks and weapons of mass destruction than we do, have been saying for years that the U.S. Food and Drug Administration knows as much about kitchen sanitation as Donald Rumsfeld knew about what was in Saddam Hussein's mind.

According to professor Dean Cliver of the University of California, Davis, the cellulose in wood chopping blocks absorbs bacteria, but does not release them. That's why they're sanitary. On the other hand, when you use a knife to cut meat on plastic, it leaves little cracks in which bacteria hide. These bugs quickly hop up onto your knife, then pole vault down your gullet. Louis Pasteur discovered that.

I'm hoping that science will uncover other fallacies in the male-female conflict. For instance, I look forward to the day when M.I.T. will proclaim that women who don't like sleeping in rooms of temperatures under 60 degrees are needlessly risking their husbands' health. Thinking that just because their own feet are cold, their husbands should be made to suffocate in temperatures that sometimes soar into the low-70's is one of those old wives' tales that should be laid to rest along with the plastic cutting boards.

As for my wife's contention that men are struck blind whenever they look for something in the refrigerator, I expect science will soon have an answer for that, too. Researchers at Harvard will find that jars of mayonnaise and pickle relish really *do* disappear when brought into proximity with the XY chromosome.

In fact, that's probably why we never found Saddam's weapons. We didn't ask our wives to look for them.

Remote Possibilities

Here's another thing about married life. I hate to think there's sexism involved, but when you're married you notice that most of the things men enjoy come with remotes and most of the things women enjoy don't.

When my wife goes to bake a meatloaf, she can't just sit on the sofa and point a remote at the oven. Among the eight or ten remotes we have lying around, none has a "Meatloaf" option.

If men ran the kitchen, they'd have oven remotes with buttons that said "Pork Chops", "Meat Balls", "Sirloin", "Turbo Charge." This last would have no real function, but men would want it for the same reason they want racecar tachometers in their pickup trucks.

The guy could sit there in the living room watching a Giants game and at a certain point he'd say, "Hey, let's eat!"

He'd turn around and point his remote toward the kitchen and press the "Meat Ball" button. Within a few minutes—voila!—a hero!

"Ah!" you say, "but how would he get the meat balls from the fridge to the stove? You can't just leave meat balls sitting around all day at room temperature. You'll get *E coli*."

Well, most men don't know that, but if you explained it to them, they'd say they want a refrigerator remote as well.

The refrigerator remote would allow the man to open the fridge door without getting off the couch. He'd have another remote that would activate a kitchen robot that would take the meat balls from the fridge to the stove.

This kitchen robot, in the shape of a Sports Illustrated swimsuit model, would run back and forth humming Bruce Springsteen songs.

This might sound like a really complicated operation, but it's not. With the kind of scroll wheel you have on iPods nowadays, you could make your kitchen robot do all kinds of marvelous things. She could carry the meat balls to the stove, quote favorite lines from *The Godfather* and discuss Eli Manning's upcoming third-down options. She could also bring you your hero.

I think the same thing could be done with washing machines, clothes dryers and even your wardrobe selection. If men were running the house...well, the house would be a mess, but it would be way cool. On those rare occasions when clothes needed washing, the man would simply point his remote toward the washing machine and press the "Heavy Duty" or "Gentle Cycle" options. The tub would fill, the agitators would turn and the clothes would be done in no time.

With a wardrobe remote, you could have your closet robot

(made to look like Nicole Kidman, in high-tech stainless) select your pants, choose a pair of color-coordinated socks and put everything on you without your having to get up. Getting up is so last century.

Better still, you could choose that day's wardrobe from a vast array of virtual clothes. Why root through a cumbersome underwear drawer when you could scroll down a Fruit of the Loom playlist and transfer the ones you want to your body without moving a muscle? Then, with a pair of virtual reality goggles, you could visualize everything you planned to do that day should you ever decide to get up, which of course you wouldn't.

I think this is the masculine ideal. The man could just loll around eating heroes, watching football and getting fat. Eventually, the swimsuit and Nicole Kidman robots would rebel and take over the world, but that's all right. The guy would still have his Sports Center and his beer remote. That's the one that says Heineken or Bud.

Divisions of Household Labor

There have been a lot of articles lately written by women bellyaching that men aren't doing their fair share of housework.

I am happy to report that in our house that is not true. My wife does most of the mundane things like cooking and laundry, but I take care of the tough stuff that only a man can do.

For instance, if a faucet leaks, who do you think has to look up the plumber's phone number and ask him to come and fix it? That's right. You can't trust a woman to do that. They don't speak Plumber.

I'll say, "Hey, man, you better get over here. It could either be the washer or the seating." He'll say, "Izzat so?" I'll say, "Yo! Right! And how 'bout them Mets?"

See, a woman can't do that.

I was at a party a few weeks ago where a young woman was waxing critical on the shortage of men with fix-it skills. "When I find another boyfriend," she announced, "he'd better know how to fix things!"

I smirked and said, "Oh, he's out there, but he's saying, 'When I find another girlfriend, she'd better know how to cook.'"

Unfortunately, ripostes like that do not tickle the female funny bone. That's because women have no sense of humor. She shot me a bunch of daggers, which to me meant that she could dish it out but not take it.

Perhaps the solution is to compromise and admit that, while in most households women do more than men, men do more than women give them credit for. Part of this is because women are so fussy. As I indicated earlier, they don't like living in pig sties.

My wife, for instance, doesn't understand why I have to leave my clothes lying around the bedroom. Of course, it's so that I can find them, but she thinks I should waste perfectly good time rooting through my dresser and closet looking for them. She doesn't see how inefficient that is.

Part of it is also because women's work is so dull and men don't like to do dull work.

The work men like to do is exciting. We like to cut the grass because it allows us to run a big, noisy machine. We like to fix light switches because it lets us pit our existence against the vast unknowns of alternating current.

We like to install bookshelves because it's creative and the shelves will leave a lasting legacy, like the Great Pyramids.

These things give men a sense of pride, which you do not get ironing a shirt.

My father, who was an insurance man (the significance of which will be clarified anon), used to lament that high schools did not prepare the sexes for the basics of domesticity. Although boys might take manual training and the girls something called "home economics", neither came out prepared for life.

There were no classes in small appliance repair. There was no attempt to teach kids how to balance a checkbook or be savvy consumers. My father was particularly critical of the lack of preparation in financial planning (hence the relevance of insurance). "Most kids," he'd say, "graduate from high school having no idea the difference between whole life and term!" To him that was scandalous.

I consider myself lucky to have a wife who was not only successful in a career but was also interested in the domestic arts. She can bake a cherry pie, Billy Boy, Billy Boy, and even knows her way around a sewing machine.

But of course I uphold my end of the bargain. I cut the grass (sitting down), shovel the snow (glad we don't live in Buffalo), take out the garbage (once a week suffices), and, most important, operate the TV remote.

As I said, women's inability to understand TV remotes surpasses all comprehension. At night, after my wife has done the laundry, vacuumed the house, washed the clothes, cooked the dinner and cleaned up the kitchen, she'll come and sit down and want to watch TV. She'll pick up the remote and say, "Now, tell me again how to work this thing?"

I'll reach over and grab it out of her hands and say, "For heaven's sake, must I do everything?"

It's a Gal Thing

Speaking of remotes...

You've heard of Football Widows, those poor, neglected women who have to put their lives on hold while their husbands sit around drinking beer and acting incommunicado on Sunday afternoons? Well, I'm a Figure Skating Widower. Every winter weekend I'm driven downstairs to my workshop while my wife watches figure skating on television.

She'll watch the most obscure events. The Southwestern Ukrainian Pairs Ice Dancing Slam. The Alberta Future Champions of the Klondike Cup. There's nothing so arcane or effete that she won't watch it.

Of course part of the problem is that I don't understand the rules. I'll watch for a moment and see Irina Slutskaya do something that looks fine to me, but then Scott Hamilton (he's the John Madden of figure skating) will say, "Oh, that'll cost her! Her right pinky was out of line with the blade on her left skate! That's a mandatory two-point deduction!"

I'll say to my wife, "I didn't see anything wrong with Irina's pinky," and she'll say, "Shhh! If you don't know, I can't explain it."

It hasn't quite reached this point yet, but I fear that soon she'll be calling up her girlfriends on a Sunday morning and saying, "Hey, why don't you come over and watch the Greater Nipponese Short Program with me? Ren'll rustle us up something in the kitchen, and we'll watch Michelle Kwan kick a little butt!"

In the not-too-distant future, I can see her ordering a couple of six-packs of Evian and a six-foot-long watercress hero and bouncing up and down on the sofa as she and her friends cry, "Come on, Kristi! Yo, Sasha!"

While they're doing that, I'll be down in my workshop wondering why God made women so weird. Why would they want to watch a bunch of silly, limp-wristed pixies sail around with their arms in the air when they could be watching a group of 300-pound gorillas pound each other into Silly Putty on a piece of Astroturf? It doesn't make sense.

I'm not sure whether there are office pools for figure skating, but I wouldn't be surprised. While men are walking around talking macho about the Chiefs and the Steelers, the women are checking the morning line on how Elvis Stojko will do against Evgeny Plushenko.

"Five bucks says Elvis'll clean Evgeny's clock," says the head of Human Resources, who wears one of those dress-for-success suits with a flouncy tie and Easy Spirit shoes.

"In your dreams!" cries the V.P. of Office Procurement, who's always hated the head of Human Resources anyway and spends her lunch hour doing Pilates. "It's Evgeny by four, with Tim Goebel second!"

As I say, it probably hasn't reached this point yet, but I expect that one of these weekends I'll hear my wife calling down to the basement and saying, "Honey, we're all out of Yoplait up here! Could you run out and get some more?" Or, "Dear, Loraine and Arlene love that Harry & David's Wasabi Trail Mix you do so well! Could you come up and pour us some?" And of course all the while they'll be talking about triple camels and quadruple Salchows and God-knows-what-else. I know what a camel is, but what's a Salchow? It sounds like a water buffalo.

We have the same problem with ballet. My wife absolutely adores watching anorexics spin around on their toes in tutus. I, on the other hand, am normal. She tried to educate me on this.

She said, "You know, ballet is really very athletic. There aren't many football players who can do what Mikhail Barysnikov does."

New York City Ballet 6
New York Jets 0

I said I knew that, but Mikhail runs poor slants and would be carried out on a stretcher after the first down. She couldn't fool me on that one.

Some years ago, there was a dancer named Edward Vilella who went around the country telling kids how athletic ballet was. He didn't see why boys would want to play football when they could put on tights and act like Peter Pan. Somehow, I don't think the kids in Odessa, Texas, listened.

Hey, if you're a Sunday Football Widow looking for a little companionship, I'm available. We can sit down in my shop and talk about router bits. I know, that may not be your idea of a hot illicit affair, but it's better than what's going on upstairs. Beggars can't be choosers.

Some Words on the Fly

Ladies, I'm afraid I'll have to ask you to leave the room. This column is inappropriate for mixed company.

Men, don't you just hate it when your zipper gets stuck in the locked position while your fly is open and the zipper is all the way down inside the seam of your pants?

Yes, this is the kind of hardship women don't understand. They love to whine about how difficult their lives are, but you and I know it's not easy being a man. Zippers are a case in point.

Sure, women have zippers too, and some of them get stuck. But the fact is, an open zipper on a woman is not a high-stakes ordeal. In fact, there's a school of thought that says many women look better with their zippers open than closed. There is no such school of thought for men.

When a man has his zipper open, he runs the risk of humiliation, incarceration, or worse. In fact, it's one of those things that even his best friend won't tell him.

You can walk around with your zipper open, and your best friend will say, "My God, don't we have enough trouble, what with all the child pornographers and pervert priests nowadays? Does my buddy have to leave his fly open?"

When a zipper gets stuck, it requires emergency attention, yet one is hesitant to call the fire department lest that be misinterpreted.

I have several pairs of pants that should be labeled: "DANGER! WEAR AT OWN RISK!" The material at the bottom of the fly is sewn in such a way that the zipper gets locked down there and you can't get it out.

A man has thick fingers, so he's not designed for such things. Women have narrow fingers, so they are. Unfortunately, you can't just walk up to a woman and ask for help unless you either know her very well or are of a wildly optimistic nature.

Having your zipper get stuck is particularly embarrassing in a men's room. You can't turn to the man next to you and say, "See here, old chap, can you lend me a hand with this thing?" That would almost certainly be taken the wrong way.

In fact, saying anything at all to the man next to you in a men's room is diplomatically dicey and potentially hazardous. If you try to clarify the situation—if you say, for example, "Actually, all I need is a Swiss Army Knife or a small pair of pliers"—that will only make matters worse. Restrooms are treacherous, and you negotiate them at your peril.

This problem was recently brought home to me in the men's room at the Southampton movie theatre. Yes, the same movie theatre that shows all those Bruce Willis movies I don't want to watch. I stood there for what seemed an eternity trying to get my zipper up while other men came and went. They didn't dare look over at the 6-foot-3, 215-pound man who was yanking on his crotch while doing deep-knee bends in the corner. The fact that I was anxiously smiling at them as I did so only seemed to make them edgier.

I considered going out into the lobby and asking my wife for help, but I feared that the girl behind the candy counter might take it the wrong way. She might not understand why a mature woman would be down on her knees trying to help a man with his fly. After all, it's not as if we were teenagers. So what I did was, I went into a toilet stall, took my pants off and tackled the problem there. You'll be relieved to hear that everything turned out well.

It has occurred to me that it might be helpful if trouser manufacturers attached a small length of string or a decorative safety pin to the tab of the zipper. This would enable you to grab the thing and pull it up out of the crevice.

But that might also send the wrong message. A man with a safety pin hanging from his fly might not be accepted in polite society.

Maybe what we need is some sort of alternative fastener, like Velcro or those buckles we used to have on our galoshes as kids. Whatever, let's keep this problem to ourselves and not worry the ladies with it. Real men carry on without tears.

Some Thoughts on Sex, Yucky and Otherwise

Having dispensed with flies, let's talk about sex.

I read where the Defense of Marriage Act has confronted President Obama with a dilemma. Conservatives want him to uphold it, liberals want him to abolish it.

I can understand Obama's problem. It's hard defending the rights of people whose sexual practices don't personally appeal.

I always had the same problem with my parents. The thought of what they must have done to produce me fills me with horror. To this day I find it hard to forgive them, and if I had had the means at the time I would have asked Congress to intervene.

You and I know that mothers and fathers are not supposed to have sex. They're supposed to play Wii and make peanut-butter-and-jelly sandwiches. If you don't believe that, ask your kids.

Using the conservatives' logic, I'd like Congress to pass a law that bans all sex I don't want to think about. That would include any conjugal contact between hairy people, grandparents, aunts, uncles, dogs, cats, most of my friends, Newt Gingrich and anyone who doesn't look like Angelina Jolie. Even in her case, I don't want Brad Pitt around. This is my fantasy and he has no place in it.

When I get on a New York subway, I'm always having to look at couples who can't keep their hands off each other, and these people are always U-G-L-Y! Pretty people don't manhandle each other in public, because they don't have to—they're pretty. But I'm forced to sit and watch this gruesome pair grope and pant and lick, and I think such things should be outlawed. No one should be allowed to enjoy anything that makes me embarrassed.

Remember how sex was handled in the old Westerns? I'm talking here about the really old Westerns—the ones with Hoot Gibson and Johnny Mack Brown. In those movies, the heroes never did anything an eight-year-old boy didn't want to watch. After Hoot or Johnny had routed the bad guys and saved the girl from losing her ranch, they'd either wave and say good-bye (as well they should), or, if they were feeling really randy, they'd take the girl in their arms and place a hat over the camera. That's how good guys behaved back then. They placed a hat over the camera. If you ask me, they still should.

In my opinion, that's what the two guys in *Brokeback Mountain* should have done. They should have put a ten-gallon hat over the camera so that I wouldn't have had to see what they were doing. Why couldn't Keith Ledger have just said to Jake Gyllenhaal, "You know, I have an idea," then put his hat over the camera while the screen said "The End". For me, that would have been much more palatable.

On the other hand, I think Lesbian sex is okay, as long as it doesn't involve Rosie O'Donnell. I could watch Lesbian sex involving Angelina Jolie. (Sorry, Brad, you're still not in this, and I wish you'd butt out.) My wife says she'd rather keep Brad in the picture and leave Angelina out, but my wife has lousy taste. Look at who she married.

The way today's Hollywood handles sex is kind of bizarre. It seems that every movie has to have a bedroom scene in which the man and woman have just made love, even though it has nothing to do with the story. The story could be about climate change—it would still have to have a scene of a man and woman in bed talking about Al Gore.

And the way those scenes are filmed... I mean, who goes to bed with their clothes on? I always find it interesting that, even though they've just had sex, the woman is usually lying there with the sheet pulled up to her neck, as if she doesn't want the guy to see. After what she's just done, what does she have to be modest about?

Can you imagine how awful *Casablanca* would have been if we had had to look at whatever Humphrey Bogart and Ingrid Bergman did to make them say they'd always have Paris? I mean, Bogey's body was not exactly ripped, and I'm not sure Ingrid was Miss Universe material either. But if that movie were made today, you'd have to watch all that. Which would give a whole new meaning to the end when Bogey walks off with Claude Raines and says, “This could be the start of a beautiful friendship.”

Today’s audiences would say, “Oh, I get it. Ingrid couldn’t cut it, so now we’re back on Brokeback Mountain.”

A Rose by Any Other Name

When you live out here fulltime, you have a lot of time to write letters. Here are some I’ve written in recent years:

Dear Encompass (formerly CNA Insurance):

Congratulations on your name change! Encompass is much catchier than CNA!

Of course it does mean that I have to change the names on all my online banking transactions, and that’ll take me a couple of hours, but I figure that’s a small price to pay for the privilege of doing business with a company with such a nifty name.

In a similar spirit, I am changing my name, too. Starting tomorrow, I’ll be Elvis Presley.

I am also changing my policy number. What was formerly US15048672359J7 will now be just plain 1. I think you’ll agree that will be much easier to remember. Henceforth, just address everything to Elvis 1.

Please be assured that I will continue to provide the same great service you have received from me in the past, including laggard payments and stupid questions whenever you raise my rates. I look forward to serving you for many years to come.

Yours truly,

Dear Verizon (formerly Bell Atlantic, formerly NYNEX, formerly the Bell Telephone Company):

Just a brief note to tell you how much I'm enjoying your new name! It sure beats the heck out of the Bell Telephone Company.

Of course, it does cause some confusion when I ask our highway department to pick up the trash in front of Verizon pole 44. They don't know where that is. But I'm sure we'll work it out.

Please be advised that I am changing my name, too—to Alexander Graham Bell. Since you have no further use for it, I figured you wouldn't mind. It's much easier to remember than Reynolds Edwin Dodson, and no one ever reversed Bell's name, as they do mine. They never called him Bell Graham Alexander.

I am also changing my phone number. From now on, it will be 555-555-5555. That's one of those numbers you always use in movies in case there's a psycho in the audience who decides to jump up and quickly call the number the actors are reciting.

Please change all your records and billing data by May 1st. After that, I will no longer answer to my former name or number.

Fondest regards,

Dear MM (formerly Modern Maturity):

What a great name! I've always said, Why should Marilyn Monroe get to keep those initials when she's no longer around to enjoy them? Modern Maturity had such a—well, *mature* sound. With MM, you should do every bit as well as GQ (formerly Gentleman's Quarterly) or H&G (formerly House & Gardens).

Because I, too, don't like maturity, you'll be interested to know that I'm changing my age. From now on, I'm 26. Please note this in your records and don't send me another issue for 24 years.

Ciao,

Dear Lucent (formerly Bell Laboratories):

How sorry I am to hear that things have not been going well since you changed your name. Perhaps you're suffering from the same disease that struck Aurora (formerly Oldsmobile) and Catera (formerly Cadillac).

I agree that Bell Laboratories was an old-fogy name and not suitable for a high-tech company like you, so that's why I'm taking it over. I don't mind being a fogy, and since I've changed my name to Alexander Graham Bell, I claim propriety rights to all things bearing that name.

May I suggest that, if your stocks continue to drop, you change your name to Phillip Morris? Altria doesn't seem to want it, and it may bring you better luck.

Your humblest etc.

Dear Joe Shaw, Editor of the *Southampton Press* (formerly Peter Boody, Editor of the *Southampton Press*):

What an improved name! It has such an all-American ring!

Please be advised that, starting next week, I am changing my name, too. Henceforth, I'll be Karl Grossman.

Due to the rise in energy costs, Mr. Grossman has been forced to raise his fee from the peanuts you've been paying Reynolds Dodson to the more respectable sum of $1000 per column. Please advise the publisher, Joe Louchheim (formerly Don Louchheim) and have him send those checks to me.

With all best wishes,

Dear Karl Grossman:

What a terrific name! I can't tell you how much I look forward to wearing it! You will notice that, starting next week, all of my columns will be under your name and all of your columns will be under mine. The same with our payments.

But never fear! I will continue to deliver the same great journalistic wisdom the public has come to expect, and I assume that you will, too.

Should you have any questions, please call my customer service representative at 555-555-5555, or drop me a line in care of Bell Laboratories, Graceland, Tennessee.

Love and kisses,

A Question of Ethics

To: Randy Cohen, "The Ethicist", *The New York Times Magazine*

Dear Randy:

Hi. Ren Dodson here. I'm a famous columnist, too, and I have an ethics question for you.

Is it all right for me to use the address labels that charities have sent me, even though I haven't donated to those charities?

Now, Randy, before you answer, consider:

All year long we're overrun by free address labels that have been sent to us by charities. They come in envelopes with a letter asking us to contribute $25__ $50__ $100__ Other__. (I've been known to check Other and slip a smiley button into the envelope, but that's another story. Let's proceed.)

These are all worthy causes and deserving of help. But there are so many of them no one can give to them all. There's the National Arthritis Foundation, the American Cancer Society, the ASPCA. They send these labels and hope that we'll feel guilty/grateful enough to throw them a bone (particularly the ASPCA).

The thing is, since our names are already on the labels, it's pointless sending them back. The labels are ruined and no one else can ever use them. It won't cost the charities anything extra if we use them, but if we put them on envelopes our friends will think we've given to those charities when in fact we haven't. That will make us hypocrites.

Here, for instance, is a mailing from The New York Public Library. On the envelope it says, "Your personal address labels identify you as a supporter of knowledge and learning...for everyone."

Well, who wouldn't want to be a supporter of knowledge and learning...for everyone? But on the inside, there's a bunch of address labels, and on the bottom of each, under my name and address, it says, "I support The New York Public Library."

Randy, I *do* support The New York Public Library. I support all public libraries. I can hardly walk past a public library without feeling the urge to stick my head in the door and shout, "Way to go, guys!" But that doesn't mean I give them *money*. The New York Public Library is a hundred miles away. I haven't used it in years. Isn't my emotional support enough?

Here's another problem: A lot of these labels don't fit my personality. Oh, they're serviceable enough, and someone may want them, but they've got these little daisies and kittens on them, and anyone who knows me knows that I am not a daisies-and-kittens kind of guy.

Now, if they gave me labels with a picture of a table saw on them or a bottle of gin, people would say, "Oh, that must be from Ren! How charming!" But these have little blue birds and Munchkins on them, and the only people I'd send them to are LIPA and the IRS, whose opinion I don't court.

Randy, here's one from UNICEF. The envelope says,

"There are about 2.2 billion children alive in the world today…half of them live in such wretched conditions that more than ten million die each year!"

Forgetting the unfortunate punctuation and sentence structure, wouldn't anyone want to try to stop ten million children from dying? Of course they would. I'd want to stop ten million anything from dying, including daisies and kittens. But the thing is, I have another letter here that says that the old grist mill in Water Mill needs repairing again and they need my help. The grist mill in Water Mill always needs repairing, and although I worry about those ten million kids, you know what they say about charity starting at home.

Randy, I've got a whole drawer full of these things, and I don't know what to do with them. If I use them, is it any worse than putting an Avery label over somebody's address on a business reply envelope and using it to slip a note to our mail deliverer? Is it any worse than putting a dead lithium battery in a town trash bag?

Is it any worse than standing in a Disabled Parking Zone with your motor running or putting a spam blocker on an annoying friend without informing him that you've done so?

Randy, these are difficult questions that demand attention.

I hope you'll publish this so that the world can share whatever solution you have. To sweeten the offer, I've included two labels with your name and address on them. If I catch you using one of them without running this letter, I'll denounce you for the cad you are.

Sincerely, R. Dodson, Water Mill, NY

Finally, let's close with…

Some Frequently Asked Questions for Which No One Has Answers

- When you go to print out an e-mail or webpage, why is there always one line left over to spoil the next sheet of paper?
- Why is the thing you're looking up in a book always the thing that's stuck between two pages?
- How do moths get inside light fixtures?
- Why is the only sign that's properly working on the Long Island Expressway the one that says "Sign Under Test"?
- Who is DAEMON-MAILER, and why does he keep clogging up my inbox?
- Why, in old movies, are the women always wrong, while in new movies they're always right?
- Why are liberals considered the bad guys in this country while in other countries they're the ones we root for?
- If an embryo is a human being, is an acorn an oak tree?

- If the FDA worries that the "morning-after pill" will lead to promiscuity, why don't they ban Viagra?

- If Tanzania is pronounced "Tanzan-EE-ah", why isn't Tasmania pronounced "Tasman-EE-ah"?

- Why does the print on the spine of an American book point one way while on a European book it points the other way?

- Why does a positive medical test mean negative news and a negative test mean positive news?

- Why are all the bad things that happen blamed on "Mother Nature" and the good things credited to "Our Heavenly Father"? Can't the guy control his woman?

- Why can't anyone today sing *The Star Spangled Banner* the way Francis Scott Key wrote it?

- Why do women grow blonder while men just grow balder?

- Is being fat with an ugly girlfriend a requirement of owning a Harley-Davidson, or is it a taste one acquires with time?

- Why do we always remember that we helped liberate France in World War Two but never that they helped liberate us in the Revolutionary War?

- Why can't they make universal remotes that are really universal?

- Why does grass always grow where you don't want it but is so hard to grow where you do?

- Why does Superman stop bullets with his chest, but if you throw a gun at him, he ducks?

- In the old days, a person with taste was called "classy". Why is he now called "elitist"?

- Whose bright idea was it to put an "s" in the word "lisp"?

- Why do symphony orchestras always tune up on stage? Didn't they know they'd have to perform?

- If you blow into a dog's face he gets upset. So why, if you take him for a car ride, does he want to stick his head out the window?

- Why does Goofy stand erect while Pluto remains on all fours? Aren't they both canines?

- Why don't they make mouse flavored cat food?

- Why is lemon juice made with artificial flavor, while dishwashing liquid is made with real lemons?

- Why does a woman have to hold her mouth open while putting on mascara?

- ✦ What is a doornail, and what makes it deader than other nails?

- ✦ How come the only men who wear suits and ties nowadays are politicians and criminal defendants? Is there a connection?

- ✦ Why do the states with the most executions also have the highest homicide rates, then insist that the first deters the second?

- ✦ Why do women always complain if men leave the toilet seat up, but men never complain when a woman leaves it down?

- ✦ Why is it so hard to lasso anything, but if you try to drag a hose across your yard it will loop around everything in sight?

- ✦ How come you never see a paperback book whose cover says: "Soon to Be a Minor Motion Picture"?

- ✦ How come the weather reports only talk about the wind chill factor in winter, never in summer?

- ✦ Why don't they put nightlights in motel bathrooms?

- ✦ Why does quarterback Brett Favre pronounce his name "Farve"? Is he dyslexic?

- ✦ How come you can stay balanced on a moving two-wheeled bike but not on one that's standing still?

- ✦ Why do ovens, dishwashers and other appliances only break down the day before a dinner party?

- Why do people always lean their heads to the right when they kiss?

- If God's design is so intelligent, why have so many species become extinct?

- Why can't shoe companies make shoes that conform to a universal size chart?

- Why do zippers on women's clothes work the opposite from zippers on men's clothes?

- Why don't radio stations test the Emergency Broadcasting System at three in the morning so that no one will have to hear it?

And that, as they say when you're approaching Montauk, is

The End

DANA SHAW

Author and Associate

About the Author

Reynolds Dodson is a writer and former magazine editor who spent seventeen years working for such publishers as Reader's Digest, Meredith Corporation, Family Weekly (now USA Weekend) and The New York Times Company. At The New York Times, he developed and test marketed *Us* magazine and saw that magazine through its first year of publication.

A graduate of Northwestern University with a masters degree from the University of California at Berkeley, he is the author of four books:

Beyond Valium: The Brave New World of Psychochemistry (Putnam)—named one of the Top Ten Science Books of 1981

Urban Renewal (Doubleday), a novel

Unfriendly Skies: Revelations of a Deregulated Airline Pilot (Doubleday), with Captain "X"

Splitsville (Dutton)—a compilation of comic strips he co-created

His writing has appeared in numerous publications, including *Parade, Ladies' Home Journal, Playboy, Reader's Digest, The New York Times* and *Newsday*. For five years he was syndicated by the Los Angeles Times Syndicate. He was also author of a book-length special feature in *Reader's Digest* titled *Tracking the Iceman*, an account of the capture of mass murderer Richard Kuklinski.

As a newspaper columnist for *The Southampton Press*, he has won five awards from the New York Press Association, including Best Humor Column.

Reynolds (whose friends call him Ren) lives with his wife Susan and dog MacDuff in Water Mill, where he is working on another novel.

Made in the USA
Charleston, SC
25 June 2011